THANK-YOUS

I would like to thank this fearless group who helped with the book. Though as children, they weren't ALL so fearless...

Adam Stower, *my illustrator*, was afraid of Frankenstein's monster. After sneaking down to watch a film at his grandad's house, he was too scared to go to the toilet alone that night!

Cally Poplak, *Executive Publisher*, loved the Loch Ness Monster and spent most of her childhood holidays on the west coast of Scotland trying to will Nessie into existence.

Charlie Redmayne, *CEO*, was afraid of Mr and Mrs Hobgoblin who lived at the end of his grandparents' garden...

Paul Stevens, *my literary agent*, was most scared of mummies as he was worried that his mum would end up becoming one!

Nick Lake, *my editor*, feared the ogre that used to speak to him from under a bridge in the Lake District. (It was just his dad, which he didn't realise for an embarrassingly long time).

Val Brathwaite, *Creative Director*, was afraid of the dark and had to sleep with a night light on until she was twenty-five!

Sally Griffin, *Designer*, was petrified of ghosts, because her naughty Mum and cheeky Uncle Maurice used to tell ghost stories round the dinner table, outdoing each other!

Megan Reid, *Fiction Editor*, has always been frightened of spiders, big or small, but especially the humongous, hairy, monster-sized ones.

Matthew Kelly, *Art Director*, was afraid of the thing that sneaks under your bed after lights-out and attempts to grab your ankle if you climb out. The only way to evade it is to take a huge leap and hit the floor running. Good luck!

Geraldine Stroud, *PR Director*, was always alarmed by the scale and size of the Yeti and still has a weird fear of vast, open spaces...

Tanya Hougham, *Audio Producer*, was often found uncontrollably wailing because she was terrified she'd turn into the Honey Monster if she ate her Sugar Puffs.

Alex Cowan, *Head of Marketing*, was scared of the Daleks and would hide behind the sofa, hearing the unstable, lumbering, zapping things hysterically shrieking EXTERMINATE!

David Walliams

WELCOME TO THE WORLD OF
MONSTERS

VAMPIRE

Like a bat, the vampire only comes out at night, can fly and has sharp fangs.

GHOST

A ghost is a spirit of the dead. It loves nothing more than spooking the living.

GORGON

This monster has snakes for hair. One look at her is enough to turn you to stone.

ZOMBIE

A zombie is a dead body that has come to life. If you are bitten by a zombie, you become a zombie too.

WEREWOLF
A werewolf transforms from human to wolf whenever there is a full moon.

FRANKENSTEIN'S MONSTER
The evil Dr Frankenstein created this monster from body parts he robbed from the graveyard.

MUMMY
An Ancient Egyptian mummified pharaoh that comes to life when their tomb is disturbed.

ABOMINABLE SNOWMAN
This rarely spotted ape-like creature lives in the snow-topped Himalayan mountains.

CREATURE FROM THE DEEP
Half man and half fish, but all MONSTER!

LOCH NESS MONSTER
The greatest of all the monsters, this dragon-like creature has been spotted in the Scottish lake.

NOW LET'S MEET *THE WORLD'S WORST MONSTERS...*

CONTENTS

BAT Baby

IN A LAND FAR, FAR AWAY, where it was forever cold, stood a snow-capped mountain. At the top of that mountain, poking out of the clouds, was a Gothic castle. It looked like something from a fairy tale, but the story I'm going to tell you is no fairy tale.

No. This is a **HORROR** story.

Inside that castle lived a flame-haired girl named Amber. Amber didn't fit with her dark surroundings. She was a girl who loved to *smile*, sing and skip. The sad thing was, she had no one to play with. That was until one *stormy* night when her baby brother arrived.

Amber couldn't have been more delighted. She liked nothing more than visiting her little brother in his nursery. She would tiptoe in just to watch him sleep.

One strange thing was that he slept all day and only woke up at night. Another strange thing was his name.

Alucard.

Have you got a brother or sister named Alucard?

If you have, you win a pound.

One night, Amber reached into Alucard's cot to stroke his hair as he snored away peacefully.

"Zᶻᶻ! ZZZᶻ! ZZᶻᶻZ!"

The baby's red eyes opened wide, and he hissed.

"HISS!"

His teeth must have just come through, as Alucard revealed a set of needle-sharp **Fangs**.

"ARGH!" cried Amber.

She was so startled she dashed out of the nursery and slammed the door behind her.

S H U N T !

"Is my baby brother some kind of monster?" she asked herself.

Before she could answer her own question, she heard a shout from downstairs.

"DINNERTIME!"

It was her mother calling.

Her heart still racing, Amber skipped down the stone

staircase. She entered the impossibly 𝗹𝗼𝗻𝗴 dining room, and asked her parents, "What are we having? I bet you are eating beetroot soup again!"

"OF COURSE!" replied her mother and father, smiling.

They made a striking pair with their pale skin, red eyes and hair as **dark** as the night. The couple, too, were forever adorned in black velvet and scarlet silk. Father's particular affectation was a long cape in which he twirled around the castle like a magician performing a trick.

"You have beetroot soup for breakfast, lunch and dinner!" said Amber. "Don't you ever get bored of it?"

"NO! We adore it," replied Mother. "We have made bangers and mash for you."

"Yummy!" exclaimed Amber, sitting at the other end of the impossibly long wooden table. She tucked into her first banger, before addressing her parents.

"I just popped into the nursery to check on Alucard."

The grown-ups shared a look.

"Yes?" said Father.

"Well, the strangest thing happened."

"Don't let your mash get cold," replied Mother, slurping some beetroot soup.

"I went to give him a stroke, and—"

"So how is that new book you're reading?" asked Father, changing the subject.

"Fine!" snapped Amber. "You are not listening to me!"

"We are, dear," said Mother. "Now eat your mash."

"No! I must tell you something! Alucard has grown **FANGS?**"

The grown-ups looked at each other before bursting into theatrical laughter.

"HO! HO! HO!"

"I think it's time for bed, young lady," said Father. "You must be tired. Your mind is playing tricks on you!"

"No," replied Amber firmly. "My mind is not playing tricks on me, but sometimes I think you are!"

"Whatever do you mean?" demanded Father.

"Being in this family is weird!"

"Weird? *Weird?*" spluttered Mother, tears blooming in her eyes.

"Why do you always dress in black and red? Why do you never, ever go out in daylight? Why do you have beetroot soup for every meal? If it even is beetroot soup. Let me taste it!" said Amber.

With that, she rose from her chair and darted to the other end of the table. Before Mother could drink the last drop, Amber dipped her finger into the soup.

PLONK!

"HOW DARE YOU!"  thundered Father. "GO TO BED THIS INSTANT!" He stood up from his chair and pointed upstairs like a father from a distant century.

Amber was shocked by how angry her father was. She had never seen him like

this. Without a word, she walked out of the dining room,
slamming the door shut behind her.

BANG!

Instead of **stomping** up the stone staircase in a
huff, Amber lingered by the door and put her ear to the
keyhole.

"Darling, one day we need to tell her the truth," said
Mother.

"NEVER!" replied Father.

Then Amber heard footsteps approach the door, and
hurled herself up the staircase.

When she reached her room, she looked down at her
fingertip. It was still scarlet from the soup. She put
it to her nose and sniffed it. It didn't
smell anything like beetroot. Her
hand shaking with fear, she placed it
to her lips and tasted it. It didn't taste
anything like beetroot either.

More like rusty old pennies.

To take the taste away, she quickly
cleaned her teeth. Then she put on her

pyjamas and leaped into bed. Lastly, she pulled the covers right up over her head.

Sleep was impossible, though. Her mind was racing. A **million** thoughts were pulsing through her brain at the speed of lightning.

Why were the curtains always drawn in the house, so not a chink of daylight could make it through?

What really was in that "beetroot soup"?

Why did her baby brother have fangs?

Why was she forbidden from entering her parents' bedroom?

Why did he have such a peculiar name?

Amber was determined to do some detective work, so she slid out of bed and tiptoed from her bedroom.

Her first thought was to check in on Alucard. However, after sneaking into the nursery and peering into his cot, she realised he **wasn't there!**

"Babies don't just disappear in the middle of the night," muttered Amber to herself. "This is getting weirder and **weirder!**"

BAT BABY

Determined to find her little brother, her first stop was her parents' bedroom. A sharp turn on the doorknob confirmed what she had always suspected. The door was locked. Amber was forbidden from entering and had never, ever seen inside. So she ventured down the sweeping staircase. After peering into several empty rooms, she heard a noise coming from the ballroom. Putting her eye to the keyhole, she was met with the most astonishing sight.

Her baby brother was flying around the room!

It was like watching an owlet taking its first flight.

The baby was bumping into things...

...the chandelier...

CLINK!

...the grandfather clock...

KERLONK!

...an oil painting...

SLAM!

...the suit of armour...

CLANK!

...the fireplace...

THONK!

...the sideboard...

THUMP!

...and the wall.

BOOF!

The tiny tot then slid down the
wall and landed on the floor with a

THUD!

"NO! NO! NO!"
thundered his father. "Son!
You are **not** looking where
you are going!"

"Don't be too hard on him,
dear," said Mother, scooping
the baby up in her arms.

"Let me show you, Alucard!" said Father. With that, his feet lifted off the ground and without even so much as flapping his arms he was flying. Father was an elegant man, and his flying did not disappoint.

He soared to the ceiling,

performed a loop round the chandelier

and landed back on the floor without so much as a sound.

"Take our hands, Alucard," said Mother.

"This is your destiny!" added Father.

The baby reached out his hands. When they were firmly gripped by his parents, the three took off.

Mother was an expert flyer too!

They glided up to the top of the room.

With his free hand, Father peeled back the crimson velvet curtain and opened the window.

"Alucard!" he announced. "All of this will be yours for all eternity. Come with us. Let us show you our empire of darkness!"

And the three flew out of the window and up into the **inky,** black sky.

Amber opened the door and *dashed* into the room. From the window, she watched the three black dots disappear into the clouds.

"I was right!" she proclaimed. "My family is weird."

A part of her wanted to chase after them. She rocked on her heels in the hope that she might be able to soar off into the night too. But she had no such luck. Amber couldn't fly. Not even when she flapped her arms.

"Not fair!" she said, stamping her foot on the floor.

With the house empty, Amber set about uncovering the truth about her weird family.

She bolted up the stairs to her parents' bedroom. She thumped her shoulder into the door, determined to break in.

THUMP!

She tried again.

THUMP!

One last time, harder than ever.

THUMP!

The door still wouldn't budge, but something fell off the top of the doorframe and landed on the floor with a CLINK!

Bending down, Amber realised this was the find of the century.

A key!

Not just any key – the key to her parents' bedroom, of course.

CLICK!

She turned the handle and the door creaked open.

CREAK!

The room was dim, and instantly Amber felt a **chill** trickle down her spine.

Stepping into the gloom, she saw something that shocked her to her core.

Instead of a bed in the centre of the room, there were two coffins!

Father and Mother slept in coffins!

It could only mean **one** thing!

They were **VAMPIRES!**

No wonder they could fly!

That wasn't beetroot soup they were drinking. It was blood!

The baby was a vampire too. But why wasn't Amber?

Alucard's name had always puzzled her. She found a leather-bound book on the shelf, and an old-fashioned quill on the desk. She scribbled the letters of her brother's name on a blank page, and then played around with them.

Then it hit her like a slap in the face!

Alucard backwards spelled...

DRACULA!

Her parents had named their baby after the **PRINCE OF DARKNESS** himself, the most famous vampire the world had ever known!

"I have to get out of here! And fast!" said Amber.

She caught a glimpse of her reflection in the mirror. At the same time, she could sense someone or something behind her, but that was impossible. She turned and saw that her family was standing right behind her.

"ARGH!" she screamed.

"And what are you doing in here?" *purred* Father.

"It is forbidden!" added Mother.

"Goo-goo!" gurgled the baby.

Amber turned back to the mirror. They were nowhere to be seen. For a moment, she wondered whether her mind was playing tricks on her. She looked back to the mirror to see that they were not visible in the reflection!

Another sign, if any were needed, that she belonged to
a FAMILY OF MONSTERS!

"You are all VAMPIRES!" she exclaimed.

"You have finally worked it out!" replied Father.

"Why didn't you tell me?"

"We didn't want you to worry," said Mother.

"WORRY! That's an understatement. I am terrified!
But I have one question."

"Yes, child?" asked Father.

"Why aren't I a vampire too?"

Father and Mother shared a look.

"Because you aren't our real child,"
replied Mother softly.

"So, you aren't my actual parents?"

"No," she replied.

"I knew it!"

"We found you when you were a newborn baby. No more than a day old. Floating down the river in a basket."

"I had been abandoned?"

"Yes!" replied Mother.

"By whom?"

Father and Mother shared another look.

"Tell me the truth!" demanded Amber.

"We suspect it might be a family who live up the river," said Father.

"Take me to them! Now!" ordered Amber.

"Darling," replied Mother, "I don't think that is a good idea!"

"I said NOW!"

"We always feared this day would come," said Mother.

"Come along, then," said Father, taking Amber's hand. They walked over to the bedroom window, and he opened it.

"Let's take you home as a family," added Mother, picking up Baby Alucard and placing him under her arm.

"Thank you," said Amber.

She was lifted off the floor, and soon they were all _zooming_ into the sky. It was thrilling being up there closer to the stars, and a little part of her yearned to have vampire powers too. They swooped over the snow-sprinkled mountains until they spotted a little cottage deep in a valley, right next to the river.

Landing just outside the front door, Amber didn't want to let go of the vampires' hands.

"That was the most *magical* moment of my life," she said. "Thank you for caring for me all these years and thank you for bringing me back here in one piece."

"The least we could do," said Father.

Mother looked lost for words. She hugged the girl tight, tears budding in her eyes.

"I'm going to miss you," she spluttered.

"I'm going to miss you too," replied Amber.

"All of you!"

With that, she brought Father and her baby brother into the embrace.

The cuddle went on for an age because no one wanted to break it.

Eventually Amber pulled away. "I guess this is goodbye," she said.

"I guess it is," replied Mother.

"Goodbye," added Father, tears in his eyes now too.

"GOO! GOO! GAH! GAH!" added the baby.

Amber stepped forward and knocked on the door of the cottage.

RAT! TAT! TAT!

She looked back to where the vampires had been standing, but they were gone. All that remained were their footsteps in the snow.

As the old wooden door creaked open, Amber smiled nervously.

"Hello!" she chirped. "I am your long-lost daughter Amber!"

The door opened fully and some figures stepped out of the gloom.

It was a family of...

...OGRES!

"ARGH!" screamed Amber.

"Look! It must be that baby we abandoned!" growled one.

"Ginger hair!" agreed the other.

"She doesn't fit in here!" said a little one.

"Let's eat her!" said another.

Amber spun round and tried to run away.

Behind her, she could hear the **stomps** of the ogres' enormous feet.

The snow was waist-deep in parts, and Amber stumbled, falling face first into it.

"HELP!" she cried.

Just as the ogres reached out their giant hands

to snatch her, Amber felt herself being lifted

off the ground.

It was Mother and Father, and her baby brother.

"You're safe!" said Father.

"We've got you!" added Mother.

"Don't ever let me go!" cried Amber.

"We never will!" replied Mother.

"GOO! GOO! GAH! GAH!" agreed Alucard.

The family *soared* off into the night sky,

together once more,

heading for home.

The GHOST
of
Nightmare Park

HAVE YOU EVER been woken up after five hundred years to discover you are a ghost and that your home has been turned into a theme park?

No?

I thought not.

Well, that is exactly what happened to Lord Phantom. He had died five hundred years earlier when his head was detached from his body with an axe. That normally does the trick. He had displeased the king by serving up cold tomato soup at a royal banquet. The king did what any self-respecting monarch would do.

He had him beheaded.

"But the soup's meant to be cold, Your Majesty! It's called *gazpacho!*" were the lord's last words as the axeman brought his blade down hard on the man's neck.

SLICE!
THUMP!

The lord and his head were buried together in an unmarked grave in some woodland, such was the shame his cold soup had brought on him, his family and the country at large. Soon **Phantom Manor** became deserted, and the house and gardens fell into disrepair.

One day, hundreds of years later, the country house was bought by an American billionaire. His name was Buzz Busby. He was a little old man with a tan so orange it would make a satsuma blush. Busby's teeth were sparkling white and what hair he had left was dyed so black it was almost blue. It created quite a contrast with his face, which resembled a dried apricot. Busby had made his billions building theme parks all over America. This was to be his first one in Great Britain.

Busby named it DREAM PARK.

Then he had the most marvellous idea! The crumbling old house itself would become the site of the park's rollercoaster.

It would be called *RUINCOASTER!*

No one had ever done this before. The rollercoaster track would twist and *turn* through the old ruin's huge double doors, into the halls, down into the cellar, around the rooms and out of the windows.

ZOOM!

It would be thrilling to speed through a spooky old country house. The dust, the cobwebs, the broken chandeliers dangling from the ceilings would all add to the atmosphere.

The builders arrived in their truckloads and set to work. After months of drilling and banging, it was finally finished.

*

The instant it opened, **RUINCOASTER** became the most famous rollercoaster in the world.

It was so popular that people from all over the country queued day and night to get on it, even though the ride was over in a few seconds.

Buzz Busby wasn't a billionaire for nothing. He soon realised he had to build another rollercoaster, bigger and better than **RUINCOASTER**, to cope with the incredible demand. The problem was there wasn't a square foot of land he hadn't built on already to create a ride, a restaurant or a merchandise shop. Busby hated being a mere billionaire and longed to be a trillionaire. The only part of **Phantom Manor** that he had not developed was the woods at the end of the garden.

So, one crisp morning, Busby sent an army of diggers to clear the trees. An impossibly tall rollercoaster that reached the edge of the Earth's atmosphere, **SKYCOASTER,** was to be built there.

"I WANT THOSE WOODS COMPLETELY CONCRETED BY NOON!" he barked.

Trees were chopped down,

hedgerows were cleared

and the ground was dug up.

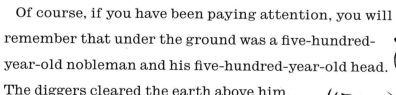

Of course, if you have been paying attention, you will remember that under the ground was a five-hundred-year-old nobleman and his five-hundred-year-old head. The diggers cleared the earth above him.

KERUNCH!

The noise woke Lord Phantom up from his eternal sleep!

Now he was a ghost!

"I say!" began his head, which was cradled under his arm, as he sat up in his grave. "What in the name of goodness are you and your mechanical beasts doing to my woodland?"

Like all ghosts, Lord Phantom glowed silver and was see-through.

The construction workers were terrified at the sight. "ARGH!" they cried.

Such was the commotion the ghost caused, that their diggers crashed into trees and each other.

BANG! KERUNCH!

The construction workers fled the woods, screaming all the way.

"HELP!"   "NOOOOOO!"

"MUMMY!"

Now, the last thing that the ghost of Lord Phantom remembered was making his final impassioned speech about the cold tomato soup. The next thing he knew, everything had fallen silent and dark. So he had no idea that hundreds of years had passed, and that his precious country house had been turned into a theme park. He didn't even know what a theme park was! A great day out for the family five hundred years ago was going to the town square to watch someone being beheaded – something that Lord Phantom and his family had enjoyed immensely until it was *his* head being chopped off.

That was **not** so much fun.

So you can imagine the ghost of Lord Phantom's shock when he stumbled out of the woodland to see his perfectly kept garden was now a thick **jungle** of rides and amusements.

The noise!

The lights!

THE PEOPLE!

"Urgh!" muttered the ghost to himself. "The place is packed with peasants!"

Of course, the biggest shock came when he entered his precious country house.

"What sorcery is this?" he spluttered, spying the rollercoaster track.

At first all was quiet, then he heard a rumbling...

RRRRRRRR!

...and he spotted a chain of carriages holding a hundred people do a loop the loop through his ballroom...

ZOOM!

"ARGH!"

...before zooming out of the window.

The ghost was swept off his feet. He dropped his head.

BOINK!

"OUCH!"

It rolled across the ballroom.

TRUNDLE!

"Pick me up, you fool!" the head shouted to the body. "I am covered in dust. **ACHOO!**"

The blind body stumbled forward, and accidentally kicked it.

THWACK! "OUCH!"

It was as if he were playing football with his own head, which is not advised.

The head came to a halt in the centre of the ballroom.

"OVER HERE!" he cried. **"ACHOO!** And don't boot me this time, you nincompoop!"

Just as the body bent over and picked up the head...

"At last!"

...the front of the rollercoaster carriage *scooped* him off the floor.

WHOOSH!

The ghost looped the loop as a hundred riders screamed behind him.

"ARGH!"

As the rollercoaster came to an abrupt halt, Lord Phantom and his head were catapulted through the air.

WHOOSH!

Shame upon shame, the ghost crash-landed in a wheelie bin.

THWUMP!

The wheelie bin lurked beside a restaurant called **BUSBY'S FINGER-LICKIN', PICKIN', FLICKIN' CHICKEN**.

So Lord Phantom emerged covered in grease, tomato ketchup and chocolate milkshake.

"The indignity!" he cried.

As he was clambering out of the bin, the ghost noticed the construction workers he had spooked earlier in the woods. They were talking to some people in uniforms with "SECURITY" emblazoned on the back of their coats. Words were tumbling out of their mouths at such a rate it was difficult to make sense of them. However, the ghost caught some of it.

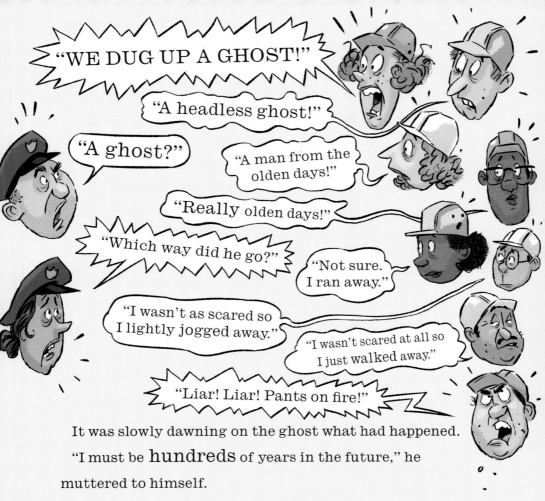

It was slowly dawning on the ghost what had happened.

"I must be **hundreds** of years in the future," he muttered to himself.

The pounding music, the kaleidoscope of lights, the forest of metal confirmed this suspicion.

"But now I hold the power! These peasants fear me! Before dawn, I will rid my home of them forever!"

Well, it didn't quite work out like that.

Let me explain...

As the ghost paraded around the park, he was delighted to witness the horror on the visitors' faces. The sight of a medieval nobleman with his head detached was enough to give everyone the willies!

"ARGH!" "HELP!"
"NOOOOO!"

Have you ever seen a headless ghost?

And I don't mean in this book, clever clogs.

No?

I thought as much.

People ran for their lives, rushing like a river through the exits of DREAM PARK.

To add to the fright, the ghost began to do peculiar things with his own head.

He hurled it up in the air...

WHOOSH!

He did keepie-uppies with it.

THUMP! THUMP! THUMP! THUMP!

He even put it on his neck upside down,

which was quite a sight.

"Run, peasants! Run!" he cried as a

coach trip of elderly people staggered

out of the exits.

Soon he was all alone in **Phantom Manor.** It belonged
entirely to him again.

"An absolute disgrace that my beautiful home has been
ruined by all these unsightly fairground novelties!"

A little part of him was intrigued, though. "I suppose I
should at least try one..." he muttered to himself. So he
approached the **Log Flume.** As the park was completely
empty, there were no queues whatsoever. He sat on the first
log and waited as it chugged up the steep slope.

"Well, this is tedious in the extreme!" he remarked.

However, after reaching the top, he finally saw where he was heading.

DOWN!

At terrific speed.

"WOO-HOO!" he cried at the thrill.

The log hit the pool at the bottom and water *SPLOOSHED* everywhere.

"Again! Again!" cried the ghost.

Because the park was deserted, the ghost went straight round again.

And again.

And again.

He ended up doing the **Log Flume** ten times in a row!

Next was the **Pirate Ship.**

This he rode fifty times!

"AHOY!"

Next, he and his head rushed to

the ***RUNAWAY TRAIN.*** Having died five

hundred years ago he had no clue what a train was, let

alone a runaway one. However, once again he went round

and round and round the track, having the time of his life.

Well, time of his death, really, because he was

a ghost.

"CHOO-CHOO!" he exclaimed, mimicking the

noise of the train.

When he'd finally had enough, he noticed the hundreds

of photographs of him on display in the booth.

"How wonderful! I have been painted to perfection!"

he said, admiring himself in various expressions of

excitement.

It was now midnight, and there was so much more of the park to discover. The ghost went on:

The Teacups!

This was one of those spinning rides that spun you round in circles. After being spun a thousand times, the ghost felt as if he might throw up that cold tomato soup, the last meal he had eaten five hundred years before. The silver phantom turned a putrid shade of *green*.

THE BUMPER CARS!

With his hands on the steering wheel and his head in his lap, the ghost could not see where he was going. That just added to the FUN. The car whizzed round the track, bumping the other cars high into the air.

The Ghost Train!

Surprisingly for a ghost, the Ghost Train gave Lord Phantom the willies. As soon as it shuddered to a halt, he ran away as fast as he could, cradling his head in his hands.

"Witchcraft! Witchcraft!" he screamed. "Begone, spirits! Begone!" Then he had a sudden moment of realisation. "I don't mean me begone. I mean the other spirits! The properly scary ones!"

By dawn, the ghost had experienced every single attraction at DREAM PARK.

"I hate to admit it," he muttered to himself as he sat on a plastic toadstool, "but I do think these additions have livened up this old place no end!"

As the morning sun rose in the sky, there was the distant sound of whirring.

WHIRR!

Lord Phantom looked up to see a helicopter slicing through the air.

"What dragon of the skies is this?" he asked himself as he rose to his feet.

The helicopter touched down on the lawn of **Phantom Manor** not far from him, and a short man stepped out.

"Good morning!" the man chirped.

"Good morrow to you! May I have a ride in your winged beast?"

"Perhaps later. We need to talk."

"Talk away, sir!"

"I am Buzz Busby."

"What kind of a ridiculous name is that?"

"An American one."

"Never heard of the place!"

Busby smirked.

"I demand to know who you are!" spluttered the ghost.

"Well, I am the billionaire owner of DREAM PARK."

"It's called **Phantom Manor!** And I think you will find I am the owner! And I am a hundredaire!"

"Please calm down, Mr Phantom!"

"*Lord* Phantom, you blaggard! I challenge you to a duel!"

"Lord Phantom, I'm sorry. But, in fairness, you died five hundred years ago. I bought this wreck and turned it into one of the greatest theme parks in the world. But now you come back to life and ruin everything!"

"It's not my fault your labourers dug me up!"

"You shouldn't have been buried there!"

"You may be shocked to discover that when it came to having my head detached from my body, I had no say in the matter!"

"Won't you just please go back to wherever you came from?"

"How dare you! I am Lord Phantom, and this is **Phantom Manor!** This is where I came from! This is my home! No! Never! Now buzz off, Mr Buzzy Buzzbuzz, or whatever your ridiculous name is!"

Being a billionaire, Busby was not used to being denied anything. His eyes narrowed. His nostrils flared. His ears waggled.

"HOW DARE YOU!" he thundered.

"I DO DARE! I DO!"

"I DARE TOO!"

"I DOUBLE DARE YOU!"

"I DARE YOU TO INFINITY AND NO RETURNS!"

Suddenly, there was a loud noise from the gates of DREAM PARK. News had spread around the world of this real-life (or rather real-dead) ghost. Now, thousands of people were flocking to the park to see this headless wonder.

"LET US IN! LET US IN!" they cried, rattling the gates.

"What do these peasants want?" asked the ghost.

"WE WANT TO SEE THE GHOST!" they chanted.

Buzz Busby's eyes lit up with glee. "I am going to be rich!" he cried. "Well, I am already rich! Richer than rich! Not just a trillionaire but a zillionaire!"

"They want little old me...?" asked the ghost, trying his best to sound humble for the first time in his life (or, rather, death).

"They do! This could be the first theme park in the world to have a ghost! It will be a sensation!"

"A sensation, you say?"

"Yes!"

"Hmm," mused the ghost. "Do I have any say in the matter?"

"If you must," replied the hard-nosed businessman. "The question is, your lordship, how would you like to be the most famous ghost in the world?"

Now Lord Phantom's silver eyes lit up with glee. "Well, since you put it like that! Open the gates. Let the peasants in!"

Within moments, Lord Phantom was **SWARMED** by thousands of people, all eager to meet an actual ghost and have their picture taken with him.

In time, Busby renamed DREAM PARK.

He called it **Nightmare Park.**

The ghost of Lord Phantom became the **STAR** attraction. People came from all over the world to **Nightmare Park** to meet him.

"Welcome to **Nightmare Park,** peasants!" he would say as he welcomed them through the gates with a smile.

Then the ghost would lie in wait, hiding among the rides. When the carriages trundled past, he would ⱨⱨⱨⱨ his head up into the air, giving them the fright of their lives!

"BOOO!"

"ARGH!" children would scream in delight.

Thanks to Lord Phantom, **Nightmare Park** became the most popular theme park in the world.

No doubt you will be pleased to learn that, as a result, Buzz Busby became a gazillionaire! The only thing people didn't like was the cold tomato soup that Lord Phantom insisted was added to the menu at **Nightmare Park's** restaurant.

That had been renamed too. **LORD PHANTOM'S FINGER-LICKIN', PICKIN', FLICKIN' CHICKEN FOR PEASANTS.**

Sometimes an unsuspecting child would try the soup. "Ugh, it's cold!" they would say.

"It's called *gazpacho!*" the lord would always roar. "It's meant to be cold!"

The soup would dribble straight out of his neck, on to the table.

DROOBLE!

My Mother
is a
ZOMBIE

ONE NIGHT, a terrible STORM ravaged the Earth –
then the unthinkable happened. All around the world
the dead rose from their graves, AND ZOMBIES

STALKED THE EARTH!

Every village, every town, every city, every country was swarming with these monsters. Zombies were easy to spot.

HOW TO SPOT A ZOMBIE

Red eyes

Pale skin

Specks of blood

Outstretched arms

Jerky movements

Unruly hair

Dazed expression

No words, just grunts

Filthy clothes

Whiff of mouldy Spam

I know that sounds a bit like your teenage brother or sister, but, no, these were definitely zombies!

The zombies had just one desire: to eat the living. Once someone had been bitten by a zombie, they became a zombie too. So the number of zombies grew and grew. If you saw one, you had to run, run, run for your life!

One lady was not so lucky. Her name was Maria. She became a ZOMBIE!

Let me take you back to the time before that. Now, Maria was a single mother, and the kindest, most caring parent any child could ever wish for. Her son, Bruno, was a very lucky boy, as she showered him with the love of not one parent, not two, but three!

Since the ZOMBIE APOCALYPSE, the mother and son had been hiding out in a caravan in a forest. Nearby was a tiny rural village named Arcadia that had yet to be swarmed by zombies. Zombies tended to stick to the cities rather than the countryside. There were far more humans to eat in built-up areas.

Once a week, Maria and Bruno would cycle into Arcadia to get some supplies. The peculiar thing about the village was that all the villagers were old ladies. Every single one. Whenever the mother and son came into the village, the old ladies kept their distance from the pair, whispered about them behind their backs and looked at them with a deep, dark suspicion. Often it sounded as if they were speaking another language, one that Bruno could never place. Sometimes, the old ladies would all squeeze into the village's mobile-library van, which had a strange habit of disappearing and reappearing in the most unlikely places. Strangest of all was that sometimes at night they would stand still all over the village, staring up at the stars.

Just as Maria and Bruno were packing up their caravan to move to another village, the inevitable happened.

A siren sounded.

WHOO! WHOO! WHOO!

"ZOMBIES!" shouted Bruno over the noise. "WE HAVE TO FLEE! NOW!"

So the pair leaped on Maria's bicycle. She pedalled and Bruno sat on the handlebars.

"Where are we going?" asked Bruno.

"The village train station! Then we can get as far away from this place as possible!"

"But where will we go?"

"I don't know yet! Somewhere where there are no zombies!"

Together they raced through Arcadia. Everywhere they looked there were zombies, zombies and more zombies!

Zombies at the **post office**

Zombies on the **bowling green**

Zombies at the **PUB**

Zombies in the **churchyard**

Zombies splashing about in the **pond**

"MUM! ZOMBIE!" shouted Bruno.

A zombie had stumbled into their path, his arms outstretched to grab them.

74

"GRRR!" he growled.

The zombie just missed them, but spun round to give chase.

Up ahead, zombies crowded the road. Maria had to steer the bike wildly to escape their clutches. Finally, the pair reached the village train station only to see that the train was already departing.

CHOO! CHOO!

"WE'RE TOO LATE!" shouted the boy.

"HOLD ON TIGHT!" cried Maria as she pedalled *faster* and *faster.*

WHIRR!

Now travelling at super speed, they had a fighting chance of making it on to that last train out of Arcadia.

But DISASTER STRUCK!

"MUM! LOOK OUT!" cried Bruno, but it was too late.

The bicycle ran over a discarded walking stick, and...

WOOMPH!

Bruno flew forward off the handlebars.

"A A A H H H !"

He tumbled to the ground with a **THUMP!**

"BRUNO! NO!" cried Maria, abandoning her bicycle to

pick him up. Cradling the boy in her arms, Maria ran as fast as she could while the zombies giving chase gained on them.

"GRRRR!" "GRRRR!" "GRRRR!"

growled the zombies.

Just like teenagers, zombies aren't great conversationalists.

"MY BOY!" cried Maria to the folk already onboard.

Helping hands reached out, and Maria passed her precious child to them.

Just as Bruno was safely on the train, Maria ran to the nearest open door, but tripped over a dropped suitcase.

TRIP!

She ended up flat on the platform floor.

THWACK!

"MUMMY!" cried Bruno. "BEHIND YOU!"

Looming over Maria's shoulder was the biggest, **baddest** zombie. The monster grabbed her by the ankle and hoisted her off the ground.

"GET OFF ME, YOU BRUTE!" cried Maria.

"GRRR!" growled the zombie.

Just as the zombie's mouth chomped down on her ankle, Maria kicked the monster away.

KICK!

It stumbled backwards, and she scrambled to her feet then leaped on to the train.

Bruno wrapped his arms round his mother and held her tighter than ever.

"Mummy! I thought I'd lost you!"

"No, no, little Bruno! I will be here for you forever!"

Bruno looked down at his mother's ankle.

"Mum! Are you hurt?" he whispered.

"No," she lied as a tiny pearl of blood trickled down her foot. The zombie had barely scratched her skin with its teeth. However, that was all that was needed to turn Maria into a zombie too!

Bruno gulped. He feared the worst. And the worst was round the corner.

The transformation happened very slowly for Maria. So slowly that when they were hiding out with the other escapees on a tiny zombie-free island in the middle of the sea, no one guessed that she was one of the **undead.** That was because she hadn't gone FULL ZOMBIE yet.

Her skin was just a little pale.

Her eyes had only a hint of red.

Her hair had become slightly unruly.

She was a trifle wobbly.

Every other word was a grunt.

Sometimes her arms were stretched out in front of her.

And there was just a faint whiff of spam about her.

While they were hiding out, they watched the island's one and only television and saw that the armies of the world had joined together to blast the undead into oblivion. Finally, the ZOMBIE APOCALYPSE came to an end. All those who were left alive rejoiced. There were no more zombies left in the world.

Except one.

Bruno realised his mother was a ZOMBIE!

But how long would he be able to keep her zombiness* secret from the world?

The pair returned to their home, the caravan in the forest. Bruno was sure that it was now the safest place for his zombie mother to be.

The problem was that there were quite a few telltale signs that she wasn't your average mum.

Bruno went to school in the next village. At the school gate as the last lesson of the day was finishing, if anyone

* This ridiculous word isn't even in the Walliamsictionary.

pushed into the line of parents, Maria's zombie brain would see red. She would lift them above her head and hurl them into a bush.

WHOOSH!

"MUM!"

If Maria attended Bruno's Saturday morning football club, she would often chase after the ball herself. All the children would be knocked out of the way, and she would kick the ball so hard the goalie would end up tangled in the back of the net.

"OOOF!" "MUM!"

Then at the end of the match she would squeeze the football between her **super-strong** zombie hands and **burst** it like a balloon.

POP!

"MUM!"

If Bruno lost a pencil somewhere in the caravan, his zombie mother would lift their home off the ground and shake it until the pencil fell out, along with everything else inside. Plates. Books. Chairs.

RATTLE!

KLUTTER!

"MUM!"

The old ladies of Arcadia were now more suspicious of the pair than ever.

Bruno would have to tell them fibs, like:

"Mum's just having a funny turn."

"Oh no! Mum always used to growl like that!"

"So sorry Mum's being a tiny bit bitey today!"

However, as his mother became more and more like a zombie, Bruno had to take desperate measures to keep her secret safe.

The boy would...

...put a kazoo in her mouth to turn the growls into musical notes...

...paint his mother's face with make-up in the morning, so she didn't appear quite so pale and deathly...

...spray her from head to toe with air freshener so she didn't smell so Spammy...

...place a tray of drinks on her arms, so it looked as if they were outstretched for a reason...

...squeeze her feet into his old roller-skates, so she glided along the pavement rather than doing her dead-giveaway zombie shuffle...

Of course, the sight of a woman in full clown make-up roller-skating through the village, carrying a tray of drinks while playing the kazoo and trailing a cloud of scent led to a great deal of gossip.

So, one afternoon, all the old ladies of Arcadia gathered in the village hall. Every single one of them had noticed there was something peculiar about Maria.

"We need to find out once and for all," said the mayoress, "whether she is a zombie or not!"

"Hear! Hear!"

So, at dusk, the old ladies piled out of the hall and into the mobile-library van. They drove at speeds of up to ten miles an hour until they reached the edge of the forest. Ready for action, these old ladies were armed with whatever deadly weapons they could lay their hands on...

Umbrellas

Egg whisks

Cheese graters

A tea strainer

A cake-tin lid

Pooper-scoopers

Used tissues

Feather dusters

Spoons

A bookmark

A pen on a chain

A cat

Inside the caravan, Bruno and his mother were happily playing chess. The boy knew it was best to let his zombie mother win. If he didn't, she tended to *snap* the board in two and eat it.

So, just as he was making a stupid move, Bruno was distracted by shadows moving outside the caravan.

"Mum? I think there is someone out there!"

"GRRR!" was her reply. She only said "grrr" these days.

It wasn't until he put his face right up to the glass that he saw the faces of the old ladies, illuminated by torches. They looked super spooky. Much spookier than his own zombie mum!

"URGH!" he cried in shock before he gathered himself together. "Mum! Stay here!" he ordered.

"GRRR!"

Bruno took a deep breath and opened
the door to the caravan.

"Good evening!" he said brightly, beaming the
biggest smile he could muster.

Sadly, the smile was not contagious. The old ladies
kept frowning.

"We need to speak to your mother!" announced the mayoress.

"She's out!" lied Bruno.

At that moment, his mother's face loomed behind him.

"**GRRR!**" she growled.

"OOOHHH!" cried the old ladies in fright.

"Oh! Hello, Mother! I didn't see you there!" chirped Bruno. "Let's get back to our chess game."

She took a bite out of a bishop.

KERUNCH!

"We have good reason to believe your mother is a…

ZOMBIE!" declared the mayoress.

"MY MOTHER, A ZOMBIE?" replied the boy. "HA! HA! HA! Whatever would make you think that?"

"**GRRR!**" demanded his mother, which didn't help matters one bit.

Then she tore off the door to the caravan and flung it over the old ladies' heads as if it were a Frisbee.

WHOOSH!

They ducked and the door hit a tree.

It hit the tree so hard that it toppled over.

THUD!

"Well, that seems to clear everything up! I wish you all a pleasant evening!" chirped Bruno. With that, he went to shut the door to the caravan, before realising it wasn't there any more.

"Not so fast!" said another impossibly old lady, hobbling out of the mobile-library van on her Zimmer frame. There was quite a wait until she'd made it all the way to the caravan.

"We will destroy your mother if it's the last thing we do!" she added.

"With that egg whisk?" asked Bruno, chuckling.

Even his zombie mother found this funny. "HUH! HUH! HUH!"

"It's not just an egg whisk!" said the old lady. "It's a **LASER** blaster!"

She fumbled with a switch on the side of the egg whisk, and a blast of red light shot out.

ZAP!

It blew a flaming hole in the side of the caravan.

BOOM!

"How come you have a **LASER** blaster? You are an old lady!"

"But I am not just an old lady. I am really an alien from the planet Xoxoxoxoxoxoxoxoxoxo!"

"What kind of a planet name is that?"

"It's better than Earth! So obvious!"

With that, she pulled off her mask to reveal a horrifying lizard creature underneath.

"Ladies!" cried the alien.

All the old ladies behind her did the same, each

revealing a face more horrifying

than the last!

"ARGH!" screamed Bruno.

"HURGH!" agreed his mother. It takes a lot to scare a zombie, but this did the trick.

"What are you going to do?" demanded Bruno of the old-lady aliens.

"We are here to take control of Earth. But first we need to destroy the human race! Starting with you two!"

Suddenly, all the aliens revealed LASER blasters hidden in their weapons. Deadly shafts of red light shot out.

ZAP!
ZAP!

The beams hit the caravan, turning it into a ball of flames.

WOOMPH!

"QUICK!" screamed Bruno. He grabbed his mum by the hand. Together they hurled themselves out of their burning home, landing on the forest floor with a

THUMP!

"GRRR!" growled the zombie as she hit the ground. Bruno leaned down to help his mother up to her feet. As soon as he had, the pair realised they were surrounded by the terrifying lizard aliens.

"Oops!" said the boy.

"Prepare to be destroyed!" said the alien with the egg-whisk LASER blaster. She seemed to be their leader.

All at once, red LASER beams shot out of all the aliens' weapons.

ZAP!

ZAP!

ZAP! ZAP!

The shafts of light burned the ground around them.

Bruno grabbed his mother's hand and pulled her behind a tree.

The lizard **aliens** came closer and closer, their weapons blasting the tree with every step.

ZAP! ZAP! ZAP!

"We're done for!" whispered Bruno.

"GRRR!" growled his zombie mother, shaking her head.

She wrapped her super-strong arms round the tree and began to yank it out of the ground.

"GRRR!"

"We can floor them with this!" said Bruno.

"GRRR!" replied his mum, nodding her head.

But, however hard she tried, the tree wouldn't come.

"Let me help!" said Bruno, but he wasn't strong enough to make much of a difference.

ZAP! ZAP! ZAP!

Still the blasts kept coming.

"SAY GOODBYE FOREVER!" taunted the closest **alien,** just a step away from the tree.

Suddenly, Bruno had an idea. A brilliant, awful idea!

"BITE ME!" he yelled.

"HUH?" said his mother.

"BITE ME! TURN ME INTO A ZOMBIE TOO!"

She shook her head.

"BITE ME! PLEASE! I BEG YOU! IT'S OUR ONLY HOPE!"

She shook her head even more.

"All right! Then I will make you bite me!" said Bruno. He put the tip of his finger inside his zombie mother's mouth and then with his other hand he tickled her under her chin.

CHOMP! went her mouth, biting down on the boy's finger.

"YOWEE!"

screamed
Bruno.

The **aliens** had now surrounded the tree. They looked on in confusion as the boy began to transform in front of their eyes.

Bruno's skin turned deathly pale.

His eyes shone red.

And he began to pong like out-of-date Spam!

But the best part was that the boy now had zombie powers just like his mother!

"GRRRRR!" he growled.

Together he and his mother yanked the tree out of the ground. They hoisted it above their heads and spun it round.

WHOOSH! It knocked over all the **aliens** like skittles.

Their weapons flew out of their lizard hands and landed far away.

Now it was the turn of the zombies to circle the **aliens.** They stretched out their arms and stumbled towards them.

"**GRRRR!**" the mother and son zombies growled together.

Without their weapons, the **aliens** cowered.

"TO THE SPACECRAFT!" said their leader.

On her order, the **aliens** all charged towards the mobile-library van and bundled inside. The van glowed bright red and transformed into a spacecraft!

CLONK! CLUNK! CLINK!

Then it **blasted** off into space.

ZOOM!

The pair of zombies on Earth looked up at the trail of fire across the night sky.

"**GRRRR!**" they growled happily.

Huge smiles spread across their faces, and they hugged each other tighter than ever.

The pair had foiled an actual **alien** invasion. They had saved the Earth!

The only downside was that they were both now

ZOMBIES!

Still, nobody's perfect.

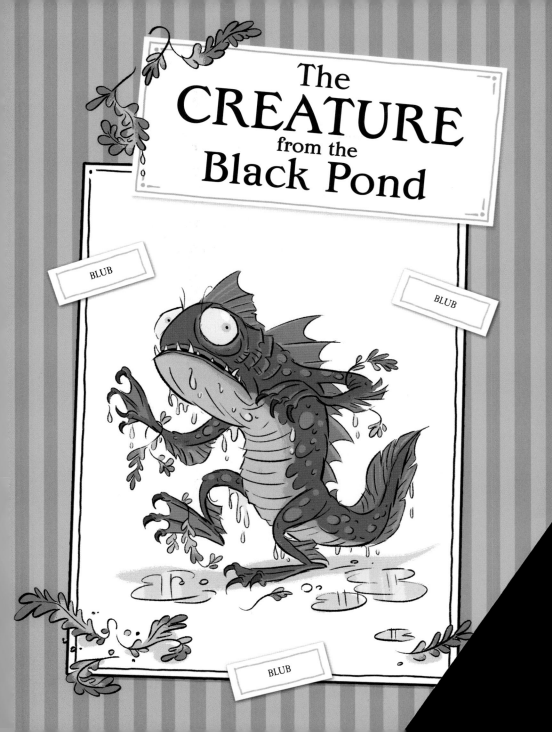

The
CREATURE
from the
Black Pond

The water in the pond had turned **black**. It
~~~~ally water any more – it was a thick, dark
~~~~ng could survive in it. The fish and
~~~~f years before. Even the waterlilies had
~~~~der the surface, never to be seen again.

The pond was just one small part of an unloved garden. It was a jungle of weeds and stinging nettles, with the tallest tree you ever did see looming at the end. The tree was barren of leaves. Just an endless knot of dead wood. It was the garden of an old country house, long forgotten in the deep, dark countryside. It had been left to rot for a hundred years, and was now a crumbling wreck. Floorboards were broken. Wallpaper was peeling from the walls. Windows were cracked or boarded up.

It wasn't really a home. But it was the only one Sally had. The girl was an orphan and had been sent to live with her grandmothers, who loathed each other with a passion.

Sometimes you have a *nice* grandmother and a **nasty** one. A nice one who gives you fudge, and a **nasty** one who then snatches it out of your hand.

Sally had two **nasty** ones.

The grandmothers lived together out of convenience. It was cheaper to share the costs of the bills, not that they ever lit the fireplaces or ran a hot bath. They could afford to: under their bed they kept old leather suitcases stuffed full of cash. They were just too **mean.**

Their names were Grandma Grub and Grandma Grot. It was easy to remember who was who.

Grandma Grub looked like an unformed **beetle.**

Meanwhile, Grandma Grot was so **filthy** a cloud of dirt followed her around like a bad smell. A bad smell followed her around too.

PONGY WONGY WOO!

These were the **nastiest** grandmas in the history of grandmadom.*

The grandmothers were **nasty** to each other.

They would put *electric* eels down each other's toilets so that when they sat down to go they received *electric* shocks on their bottoms.

BUZZ!

They were **nasty** to strangers.

If anyone dared knock on their front door asking for charity donations, they would **pelt** them with rotten eggs, then steal their collection tins.

CRACK!

They were **nasty** to animals.

If a cat dared find its way into their garden, the grandmas would **SQUIRT** water at it with the hose.

SPLOOSH!

* See your **Walliamsictionary** for this and a gazillion other bonkers words.

They were **nasty** to their friends.

Oh no. Hang on. They didn't have any friends. Grub and Grot were far too **nasty** for that.

However, they saved up all their most **nasty** nastiness for **one** person and one person only. Their granddaughter, Sally. They had taken the orphan in purely for her to become their servant. The poor girl had to do everything for her grandmothers:

Grate the **dead skin** off the bottom of their feet with a cheese grater

Pick their **noses** for them

(On her birthday, she was told she could eat the **bogies** as a special tasty treat, but Sally declined their kind offer)

Pluck the *hairs* out of their chins and then stick them in a scrapbook to save for posterity

Clean the **filth** out of their fingernails with the end of a pencil

Suck the **wax** out of their ears with a straw

Because of her grandmothers' nastiness, Sally's life had become miserable. She wasn't allowed to go to school as she "had work to do!". She was forbidden from leaving the house unless she was told to run an errand for the old ladies. The only time Sally had to herself was around midnight. All the chores would be done. Grub and Grot would be fast asleep by then. She had until dawn before they shouted at her for their breakfast in bed. So, at night, Sally would lose herself in the tangled garden. She always found herself being drawn towards the **black pond.**

Occasionally, she would witness a bubble pop on the surface.

PLOP!

Or a shape twist in the depths.

SWOOSH!

Or the sludge rise in an instant and *spill* over the sides of the pond.

SPLODGE!

Over time, she became convinced that something was living in there...

One night, something horrifying happened.

A **webbed hand** appeared out of the sludge!

"ARGH!"

screamed Sally, dashing back to the house.

She ran upstairs to the grandmothers' bedroom and without knocking burst through their door.

"Wake up! There's a monster!" she cried. "A monster in the pond!"

"HOW DARE YOU WAKE US UP!"

bellowed Grub from their four-poster bed, which was now a three-poster, as one of the posts had snapped off.

"This girl needs a good thrashing!" added Grot.

"That can wait! Please! This is serious! Deadly serious! I just saw a **monster** in the pond!"

"LITTLE LIAR!" snarled Grub.

"Thrashing's too good for her! Needs a good boot up the bottom!" added Grot.

"Listen to me! For once in your lives, please just listen to me! I'm **not** lying!"

"Exactly what a liar would say!"

"Hard to argue with that!"

"I promise! I swear on my **rotten** little life! There's a real-life monster out there! Please! Come and see for yourselves!" cried Sally.

The old ladies harrumphed and slid out of bed.

"HUFF!"

Arming themselves with a walking stick and an umbrella, the grandmothers stalked out of the house. They beat their way through the overgrown plants and **stomped** towards the pond.

Of course, now the creature was nowhere to be seen.

"So, where is this creature of yours, Sally?" grunted Grot.

"It was here! I promise!"

"We should lock her up in the dungeon for a week for getting us out of bed like this!" hissed Grub.

"I promise you, there is something down there! LOOK!"

The two old ladies peered down into the black **sludge.** It was as still as ice.

"There is nothing down there!" exclaimed Grot. "SEE?"

With that, she prodded her walking stick hard down into

the pond. Two **webbed hands** grabbed on to the end of it and would **not** let go.

"IT WANTS ME WALKING STICK!" protested Grot. "THIEVING MONSTER! WELL, DON'T JUST STAND THERE! HELP ME!"

The other two held on to Grot, but all three were no match for whatever was down there. The green **webbed hands** yanked hard on the stick.

"LET GO, GRANDMA!" cried Sally.

"NEVER! THIS IS ME BEST STICK!" snapped Grot, and she flew headfirst into the pond.

WHIZZ!

SPLOOSH!

"NOOO!" cried Sally.

Grandma Grub seemed unmoved by the apparent demise of her best enemy.

"That's a shame – I was rather hoping Grot was going to leave me that stick when she finally popped her clogs!"

"Is that all you can say?" asked Sally.

"What do you want me to say? Grot was a wicked old witch just like me. I despised her nearly as much as I despise you!"

Sally shook her head and sighed. As much as the evil pair had made her life a misery, she didn't want anyone to come to such a grisly end.

"Let's get back inside the house double quick!" barked Grub.

"Yes!" agreed Sally.

"We need to teach that monster a lesson!"

"Are you sure?"

"YES! FOLLOW ME!"

As the pair rushed back into the house, what they couldn't see was the monster rising out of the pond.

It was half man, half fish.

The creature had:

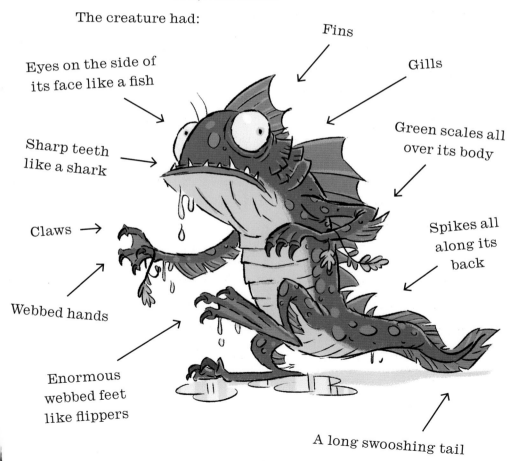

Fins

Gills

Eyes on the side of its face like a fish

Green scales all over its body

Sharp teeth like a shark

Claws →

Spikes all along its back

Webbed hands

Enormous webbed feet like flippers

A long swooshing tail

Slowly but surely, the creature from the **black pond** stalked through the overgrown garden. It followed them all the way to the country house.

Once inside the kitchen, Grandma Grub set about making sure the creature met its own grisly end.

"I know what I'll do!" she muttered to herself. "I will **blast** that creature into oblivion!"

"Please, no!"

"Oh yes!"

"But, Grandma, it's impossible anyway. We don't have a bomb."

"No, but we can make one."

"How?"

"We mix all the explosive things in the kitchen together, then *KABOOM!*"

"But we must not harm this creature!" Sally protested.

Looming outside the window was the creature, hearing every word.

"Are you BANANAS?" sneered Grub. "OF COURSE WE NEED TO HARM IT! WE NEED TO KILL IT UNTIL IT'S DEAD! NOW OUT OF MY WAY, YOU MONSTER-LOVING **FRUITCAKE!**"

Grandma Grub shooed Sally away with her umbrella and set to work.

The lady filled a **massive** pot with:

Fermenting pineapple juice that had gone all fizzy

Vinegar

An ancient tin of baked beans

Baking powder

Curdled milk

Mouldy biscuits

Custard powder

Pickled onions

Chilli powder

Stinky cheese

A banana that had long ago turned black

Grandma Grub whisked all the ingredients up together until they were fizzing in the pot. Then she poured the explosive **LAVA** into a hot-water bottle.

SLURP!

As quickly as she could, she spun the top closed.

"HA! HA!" she chuckled. "When this **explodes,** it will blast that monster into outer space!"

"Please don't!" exclaimed Sally, holding on to her grandmother's arm.

Grandma Grub whacked the girl away with her umbrella.

THWACK!

"OUCH!" cried Sally.

She was shoved aside as Grandma Grub marched out to the garden with her home-made hot-water-bottle bomb.

THE CREATURE FROM THE BLACK POND

Neither the old lady nor her granddaughter spotted who was **following** them back to the pond. The half-**man**, half-**fish** creature was only a few paces behind them as they fought their way back through the jungle of a garden.

"COME ON, MONSTER!" called out Grandma Grub at the edge of the pond, clutching the hot-water bottle that was expanding at an alarming rate. At any moment, it was going to blow. "I'VE GOT A LOVELY LITTLE SURPRISE FOR YOU!"

The creature from the pond was now *lurking* right behind Grandma Grub. It tapped the old lady on the shoulder. Slowly, she turned round.

"ARGH!" she cried.

She stumbled back and fell straight in the pond.

SPLOOSH!

Grandma Grub was still clutching the hot-water bottle, which was now a boiling-water bottle.

"GRANDMA!" shouted Sally, reaching out to save the old lady. She held on to the end of her umbrella.

"I'M GONNA YANK YOU IN TOO!" shouted Grub. She tugged hard on the umbrella, and it slipped through her granddaughter's hands.

Sally let go and the old lady disappeared under the sludge. **PLOP!**

"Creature! Can you save her?" begged Sally.

The creature took a deep breath through its gills and stepped to the edge of the pond.

But just as it was about to dive in, there was a gigantic **explosion** from the depths.

KABOOM!

It was so huge that both Grandma Grub and Grandma Grot were shot up into the air.

WHOOSH!

They were so covered in **sludge** it was impossible to tell who was who.

The pair landed at the very top of the t|ll dead tree at the end of the garden.

"WE'LL GET YOU FOR THIS, SALLY!" cried out Grandma Grot. The lady was hanging there, her nightdress snagged on the highest branch. She flapped her arms as if they were wings, which did **nothing** at all.

"JUST WAIT UNTIL WE GET DOWN!"

added Grandma Grub. Her feet were caught in a knothole near the very top of the tree. She was dangling upside down like a bat. "WE WILL MAKE YOUR LITTLE LIFE A MISERY!"

"YOU ALREADY DO!" shouted Sally.

"HELP US DOWN!"

"OR WE'LL BE STUCK UP HERE FOREVER!"

Sally turned to the creature. "It doesn't sound like such a bad idea to me!"

The creature chuckled.

"So, what do we do now?"

The creature pointed to the pond and mimed swimming.

Sally shook her head. "I never learned to swim, so an underwater world doesn't really appeal to me. Sorry. Listen, creature, because I have been held prisoner here all my life, I have never done all the things most children have done: have an ice cream, fly a kite, play football in the park!"

The creature nodded its head and smiled. It must have liked those ideas too.

Soon the pair became **best friends** and did all those things together and many, **many** more.

The creature did sometimes get funny looks, but Sally ignored those people. Had they never seen a half **man**, half **fish** before?

Together they drained the pond and filled it with fresh water. Soon, life came back to the pond. Fish swished around, frogs sunned themselves on lily pads and tadpoles darted hither and thither.

What's more, the pair had the whole house to themselves. They repaired every crack, break and hole. Over time, the old ruin became a home.

Best of all, the creature taught Sally how to **swim** in the pond. They even became a synchronised **swimming** team and took part in competitions. The judges feared the creature, so the pair always received **maximum points.**

With the creature by her side, Sally's grandmothers didn't dare be **nasty** to her. Well, they couldn't. They were still stuck up the tree. But Sally didn't want the old ladies to starve, so she sent them up lots of **yummy** food and **delicious** drinks.

Vinegar!

Chilli powder!

Mouldy biscuits!

Stinky cheese!

And **all** the pickled onions they could eat!

Food that was guaranteed to make Grandma Grub and Grandma Grot feel as if they were going to **explode.**

Sally and the creature from the **black pond** couldn't have been happier. The only downside was being kept awake at night by the noise of the ladies' thunderous bottom bangers.

KABOOM! **BANG!**

"HA! HA!" Sally would giggle from her bed.

The Legend
of the
WOLFWERE

BUSTER HAD NEVER WANTED a **pen pal.** It was his
mother who forced him into having one. The family were
on a camping trip when this **mysterious** tale begins.

"My boy Buster **loves** to write letters!" cooed
Buster's mother.

"No, I don't, Mum!" he protested.

The pair were standing outside their little cloth tent while Father was dismantling it on the campsite. He was a rather particular man with a particular moustache, and he wouldn't let anyone else meddle in such a task.

Right next door to them was an unusual family who preferred to sleep outdoors under the stars. No tent for them. Or sleeping bags. Plus, they had a big, brown, furry car they called **"the Wolfmobile"**.

"Nothing my Buster adores more than putting pen to paper. He has always wanted a **pen pal.** We must take your address so Buster can write letters every day to your little Wolfy!"

"EVERY DAY!" spluttered Buster.

"Twice a day if you like! What a good boy!"

Wolfy was the furriest little boy you have ever seen. Hardly surprising, as he came from an incredibly furry family. His father was very furry. His mother was rather furry. Even his little baby sister was somewhat furry. So they didn't need a tent to keep them warm. That thick fur kept them toasty! Their feet were furry. Their

hands were furry. Their arms were furry. Their necks were furry. Even their faces were furry. Of course, the family were all wearing clothes, but there was every chance there was fur absolutely everywhere!

Not just that...

Their ears were pointy.

Their noses were **dark.**

Their eyes were yellow and black.

Their teeth were **FANGS.**

Their tongues were l o n g and **slobbery.**

And their fingernails were claws.

They looked like **WEREWOLVES!**

On the first day of the holiday, Buster's mother had forced him to go and play with Wolfy.

"Go on, Buster!" she insisted. "The poor thing looks lonely!"

"No wonder! He looks and smells funny."

"Don't be so rude!"

"But he does! He looks and smells just like an animal!"

"Stop that! All the other children won't go near him."

"I don't blame them."

"They are cruel. I thought you were kind!"

"I am not going to play with him! And that's that!"

One morning, however, Wolfy came knocking on the door of Buster's tent. As much as you can knock on a tent.

"Hello! My name's Wolfy. What's yours?"

"Buster," muttered the boy.

"Do you want to play a game, Buster?"

"What game?"

"I have a favourite one," replied Wolfy, smiling to reveal his sharp **FANGS**.

Buster gulped nervously.

"GULP!"

Unsurprisingly, it was the game **What's the Time, Mr Wolf?** and Wolfy would always play the part of the wolf. When he turned round, he would **snarl** like a monster.

"ROAR!"

Buster would run all the way back to his tent, screaming.

"ARGH!"

So, on the final day of the holiday, Buster was looking forward to **never** seeing this strange furry boy again. Sadly for him, this was not to be...

"...And your Buster must come and stay with our Wolfy some time," said Wolfy's mother as the families were saying goodbye. "We have a lovely little remote cottage on the moors," she continued. "No one for miles and miles around. Just the moors, the mist, the howling wind, the thunder, the lightning, the ice-cold rain and the light of the silvery moon."

"AROO!" howled Wolfy.

"SHUSH!" shushed his mother.

Buster tugged on his mum's sleeve and shook his head so hard there was a very real chance it could have wobbled off.

"Oh! My Buster would love that! Maybe he could stay for a weekend?"

"NO!" protested Buster.

"All right, then, a week!" said his mother. Buster had fallen into her trap again!

Addresses were swapped and, before Buster knew it, he was being forced to pen letters to his new "pal".

The very next morning after they returned home from their holiday, a letter from Wolfy arrived on the doormat.

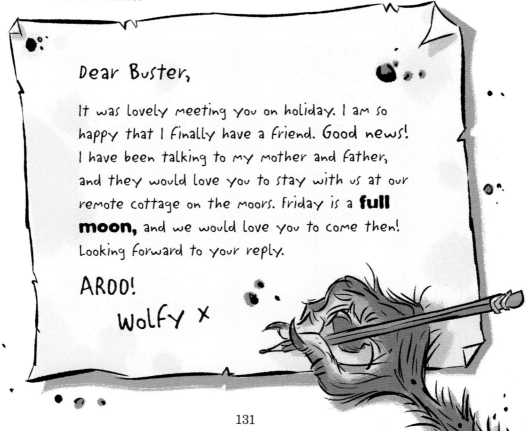

Dear Buster,

It was lovely meeting you on holiday. I am so happy that I finally have a friend. Good news! I have been talking to my mother and father, and they would love you to stay with us at our remote cottage on the moors. Friday is a **full moon,** and we would love you to come then! Looking forward to your reply.

AROO!
Wolfy x

Under threat of **never** being allowed to watch television ever again, Buster wrote back.

> To Wolfy,
>
> No.
>
> Buster

Despite this curt reply, soon **another** letter from Wolfy arrived on the doormat.

> Dear Buster,
>
> Thank you so much for your lovely letter. It was so good to hear from you, my best friend in the world. I read the letter over and over again. It brought back so many happy memories of playing together on holiday. We all look forward to welcoming you to the moors next week.
>
> AROO!
>
> Wolfy X

This was **not** the letter Buster had been expecting. He had no clue how to reply. So he just wrote...

...in big capital letters and posted it off. He was sure that he would never hear from Wolfy again. He was wrong.

Dear Buster,

Wow! I love your letters. So long and rich in detail. I don't know how you have the time to write all those words. We are so happy you, my best buddy, can join us on the moors. You will love it so much you will never come back! We don't want your parents to go to any trouble, so we will pick you up on friday evening straight after school in the Wolfmobile.

AROO!

Wolfy X

Buster was floored by this. He hurriedly wrote a reply and ran to the postbox. The letter read...

NO! NO! NO! NO! NO! NO! NO! NO! NO! NO! NO! NO! NO! NO! NO!
NO! NO! NO! NO! NO! NO! NO! NO! NO! NO! NO! NO! NO! NO! NO!
NO! NO! NO! NO! NO! NO! NO! NO! NO!
NO! NO! NO! NO! NO! NO! NO! NO! NO! NO! NO! NO!
NO! NO! NO! NO! NO! NO! NO! NO! NO! NO! NO! NO! NO! NO!
NO! NO! NO! NO! NO! NO! NO! NO! NO! NO! NO! NO! NO!
NO! NO! NO! NO! NO! NO! NO! NO! NO! NO! NO! NO!
NO! NO! NO! NO! NO! NO! NO! NO! NO! NO! NO! NO! NO!
NO! NO! NO! NO! NO! NO! NO! NO! NO! NO! NO! NO! NO! NO!
NO! NO! NO! NO! NO! NO! NO! NO! NO! NO! NO!
NO! NO! NO! NO! NO! NO! NO! NO! NO! NO! NO! NO! NO! NO!
NO! NO! NO! NO! NO! NO! NO! NO! NO! NO! NO! NO! NO! NO!
NO! NO! NO! NO! NO! NO! NO! NO! NO! NO! NO!
NO! NO! NO! NO! NO! NO! NO! NO! NO! NO! NO! NO! NO!
NO! NO! NO! NO! NO! NO! NO! NO! NO! NO! NO!

Buster was sure Wolfy would take the hint. But NO!

Dear Buster,

Splendid, my friend! That's all sorted, then.
We can't wait to see you on Friday afternoon!

AROO!   Wolfy x

As soon as Buster read it, he began to feel a deep sense of **dread.** The boy trudged home from school that afternoon, dawdling for as long as he could. When he finally turned the corner into his road, he spotted the **Wolfmobile** idling outside his house. Buster hid behind a hedge, determined not to take another step. Then he realised someone, or something, was *looming* over his shoulder. **"BOO!"** came a voice in his ear.

"ARGH!" screamed Buster.

He spun round to see Wolfy standing right behind him.

"What are you doing here?" demanded Buster.

"I was just looking for you. We need to get going. It's a **full moon** tonight, remember!"

"Um… I just need to talk to my mum!"

Right on cue, Buster's mother opened the front door.

"Buster!" she cooed, handing him a holdall. "There you are! I packed your overnight bag…"

"M-U-M!"

"Have a super weekend away!" she said, bundling her son into the back of the **Wolfmobile.**

Buster was too shocked to utter another word. All he could do was look longingly out of the back window of the car as he sat sandwiched between Wolfy and his baby sister. Their fur was tickling him, so Buster tried to make himself as small and compact as possible.

It was a long drive to the moors, and all three children nodded off on the way. When Buster woke up, it was dark. The **Wolfmobile** was winding its way through a barren landscape. Any trees still standing were dead, and a thick mist was descending. Eventually, the **Wolfmobile** came to a stop outside a cottage. It stood alone at the top of a hill, its dark grey stone making it almost invisible against the **black** sky.

WHIP!

A flash of *lightning*.

BOOM!

A rumble of thunder.

A storm was coming, and as the ice-cold rain trickled down the back of Buster's neck the family hurried inside the cottage.

It was more of a den than a house. There were no tables or chairs, just lots of fur rugs on which to lie.

"Well, I am so tired!" said Buster. "I might go straight off to bed!"

"Don't be so silly!" replied the mother. "We haven't had dinner yet! Darling?"

"Yes, my dear?" asked the father.

"Will you pop out and pick up something for dinner?"

"But there isn't a shop for miles around!" said Buster.

"Don't you worry, young sir!"

With that, the father opened the front door and stepped out into the lashing rain. Buster went over to the window and peered through the glass.

"Is he not taking the car?" asked Buster.

"He doesn't need it!" said the mother. "He'll be back before you know it! Now, you kids go off and play!"

With a heavy heart, Buster followed Wolfy upstairs to his bedroom.

He saw a *shadow* move outside the window and peered out to see Wolfy's father running across the moors, carrying a stag on his back.

"You don't get those in the supermarket!" remarked Buster.

"Nearly dinnertime!" replied Wolfy.

"Won't that thing need to be cooked first?"

"What? And lose all its flavour? No, thanks. It's so much tastier raw! Now, let's play a game."

"What game?"

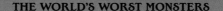

"**What's the Time, Mr Wolf?** of course!"

"Not again!"

"It will be different this time."

"How?"

"You'll be the wolf."

Buster looked at Wolfy. "I think you make a better wolf than me!"

"What makes you say that?"

"Well, Mum said not to be rude, but aren't you a were—"

"**AROOO!**" cried Wolfy.

The storm had lifted, and now the moors were lit up by a dazzling **full moon.**

"**AROOO!**"

Buster could hear hOwls coming from all over the cottage.

"I knew it!" he exclaimed. "You're a family of **werewolves!**"

"Not quite!" spluttered Wolfy as his face and body began to change. There were noises of bones stretching...

SCRUNCH!

...blood pumping...

GURGLE!

...and eyeballs swivelling.

SWOOSH!

Buster raced to the bedroom door. He tried so frantically to open it that the handle came off in his hands.

SNAP!

Now he was trapped, and he began **thumping** on the door.

"HELP! HELP ME!"

But when Buster turned back to Wolfy he wasn't **wolf-like** at all any more. He looked exactly like a

NORMAL BOY.

"What... what **are** you?" asked a confused Buster.

"A wolfwere."

"A what?"

"A wolfwere."

"I never heard of one of those."

"Nobody has. Our family are the only ones."

"How do you become a wolfwere?"

"A 'were' is an ancient name for a man."

"I never knew that!"

"A werewolf is when someone is bitten by a wolf. A wolfwere is when a wolf is bitten by a man."

"Who would do such a thing? Biting a wolf? Sounds dangerous!"

"It was hundreds of years ago now, so no one really knows who the man was. It is the stuff of **legend.** But, whoever it was, they must have been extremely hungry."

"I thought you were going to take a bite out of me!"

"No, no, no!" chuckled Wolfy. "Do you understand now why I wanted you to come and stay with us on a **full moon?"**

"So I could see you change into a boy?"

"Exactly! I know you were frightened of me."

"Frightened is a big word."

"All right, then! TERRIFIED!"

Now it was Buster's turn to laugh. "HA! HA! Was it that obvious?"

"Yep! Don't worry about it. Everyone is terrified of me. That's why I never had a friend before."

Buster felt awful to be just like all the other children who had judged Wolfy for the way he looked.

"I am sorry," he said.

"Don't be. Just give us a hug!"

Buster smiled and walked over to Wolfy with his arms outstretched. The two boys embraced.

"It feels good to have a friend!" said Wolfy as Buster's warmth tingled through him.

"It's the best feeling in the world," agreed Buster.

Just then the bedroom door opened, and Wolfy's family were standing there, all three transformed.

"We heard a commotion," said Wolfy's mother, holding the baby.

"Is everything all right?" asked Wolfy's father.

"Everything is perfect!" replied Buster.

He looked over at Wolfy and smiled.

From that night on, the two became the best of friends. By dawn, Wolfy had turned back into a wolf. He only looked like a boy on nights when there was a full moon, but Buster didn't mind having a friend that looked like a wolf one bit. It was cool! If anyone picked on Wolfy, Buster was the first to stick up for his friend.

147

That was over seventy years ago, and now the pair are both grandads. But they are still **pen pals** and write to each other every week without fail. Often, they include photographs of their grandchildren – or, for Wolfy, grandcubs!

The
Curious Case
of
MISS GORGON

THE HEADMASTER had been turned to stone!

Arthur was so shocked by what he discovered deep in the cellar of **BASKERVILLE SCHOOL** that he dropped his torch.

CLANK!

His hand shaking with fear, he picked up the torch and shone it at poor Mr Dust. The much-loved headmaster looked like a **STATUE** of himself. But it was not like any **STATUE** Arthur had ever seen before. Mr Dust's stone eyes were wide with terror and his mouth agape in what looked like a silent scream.

A scream that would be unheard for all eternity! Just as Arthur took out his magnifying glass to examine the surface of the **STATUE** for **clues,** he heard a noise in the darkness, and fled.

Arthur was the school detective. Although only twelve, he had read every Sherlock Holmes book in the library a hundred times. In honour of his hero, the genius detective, he even sported a deerstalker hat and a tweed cape. This, and his incredibly thick-lensed glasses, made him stand out at **BASKERVILLE SCHOOL.** Arthur delighted in this. He liked being special! Even if the bullies called him cruel names like MR GOOGLE. Something you should never, ever do.

Arthur's school bag was an old-fashioned leather case, packed full of all the things a detective needs:

Magnifying glass

Notepad

Pencil

Binoculars

Mirror for seeing round corners

Gloves for handling evidence

Fake eyebrows, nose and moustache for disguise

Flask of hot tea

The boy had single-handedly solved many of **BASKERVILLE SCHOOL'S** mysteries over the years. The school was a vast **Gothic** building where legends lurked in every shadow. Arthur recorded all his cases in his detective's notebook. One day he hoped they would be published, just like Sir Arthur Conan Doyle's Sherlock Holmes books.

There was:

THE CASE OF THE Missing Blancmange

The dinner lady scoffed the lot.

☑ SOLVED

The CURSE of the Lost Property Cupboard

Why did every item of PE kit that was left in there turn a putrid shade of green? Mould, of course.

☑ SOLVED

Death in DETENTION

Not a death exactly, but a little boy passed out when one of the bigger boys did a

silent but deadly bottom banger that was silent but **DEADLY** in the airless classroom.

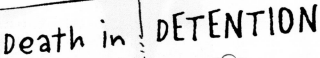

☑ SOLVED

The SECRET of the Science Laboratory

The laboratory technician had been working on a potion from all the chemicals in the cupboard to make herself invisible. She believed it was a complete success,

which is presumably why she could be spotted dancing around the laboratory holding beakers and going *"WOOH!"*

☑ SOLVED

EVIL at the Vicarage

It turned out to be just some sour milk added to the tea, but it made the poor vicar explode from both ends.

☑ SOLVED

An Appointment with MURDER

That's an appointment with Miss Murder, the school nurse. It was just a grazed knee, but, still, it made for a good title.

☑ SOLVED

However, Arthur had been yearning for a case with real drama.

Now, as he made his way quickly back up the stairs from the cellar, that case had finally arrived with his school's headmaster being turned to stone.

How could such a thing happen?

Who would do a thing like this?

And why?

Arthur was determined to crack the case!

Like all children at **BASKERVILLE SCHOOL,** Arthur was forbidden from going down into the cellar. So, even though he'd found the stone headmaster there, Arthur had to keep it a secret for now – until he had solved the mystery.

By the time Arthur finally found Mr Dust, the headmaster had been missing for more than a month. One afternoon before the man's disappearance, Arthur had been on his way up to the library when the headmaster, hurrying down the stairs, had bumped into him.

BUMP!

Sherlock Holmes books were scattered everywhere.

CLONK! CLONK!

CLONK!

Mr Dust didn't say a word. He didn't even stop. He just kept on going. Down.

Down.

Down.

It was as if the headmaster were fleeing from someone or something. By the time Arthur had picked up the last book, the man had gone. As far as the boy knew, that was the very last sighting of him.

Arthur had searched everywhere inside the vast Gothic boarding school and outside in the grounds for weeks.

Wild theories about Mr Dust's disappearance spread through the school like **NITS!**

The headmaster had stolen all the **toffees** from the tuck shop, then gone on the run to Peru where he could scoff the lot himself.

He had been **knocked out** by the stink in the Lost Property cupboard and was buried beneath a pile of PONGTASTIC pants.

He had been **shrunk** to the size of an **ant** in one of the laboratory technician's bizarre experiments.

Arthur had other theories. He had long been suspicious of the deputy headmistress. In Mr Dust's absence, she had assumed the role of headmistress. Her name was Miss Gorgon, and she was a deeply **mysterious** character. Miss Gorgon wore dark glasses, which she never, **ever** took off. Her face was caked with make-up. Her hair was completely hidden by a **large** felt hat that she pulled down low over her head. All Miss Gorgon had to do was *sweep* down a corridor, and the younger pupils would **Scatter** in terror.

So, in the assembly for Arthur's year, the boy took great interest in what Miss Gorgon would have to say on the matter of Mr Dust's disappearance. She took to the stage in the oak-panelled hall and addressed the hundred or so children.

"I know all of you must be wondering what has happened to Mr Dust," she began. "I regret to inform you that he has been taken ill. Gravely ill. So ill, in fact, that he is... dead."

There were gasps from all the children.

"GASP!"

"Miss Gorgon?" began Arthur from the back of the hall. "How did Mr Dust die?"

Hundreds of pairs of eyes *swivelled* to see who had spoken. No one else was brave enough to challenge Miss Gorgon. In one of her History lessons, a little girl had questioned why  they only ever studied Ancient Greek mythology. Miss Gorgon made her stand in the corner for an entire term. On one leg. Hopping. While juggling books.

"Ah! Arthur!" exclaimed Miss Gorgon. "I should have known it was you. Our school's very own Miss Marple!"

The children chuckled at the comparison to Agatha Christie's little-old-lady detective.

"HA! HA!"

Arthur shrugged. Miss Marple was a genius detective, just like Agatha Christie's other famous creation, Hercule Poirot. He didn't mind the comparison at all, although his favourite fictional detective was Sherlock Holmes, of course.

"If you must know, Arthur, Mr Dust came to a *sticky end* when he was involved in a rather serious **papier-mâché** accident."

There were bemused looks and low whispers from the children in the room.

"What?"

"How?"

"I am not choosing Art again next year!"

"Miss Gorgon, how exactly do you die from a **papier-mâché** accident?" asked Arthur.

"*Excruciatingly,*" she purred.

It sent a *shiver* down Arthur's spine. It sounded like a threat. It stunned the boy into silence.

"That is the end of the matter. Any further discussion on the subject is strictly forbidden. Mr Dust's demise has left me in complete control of **BASKERVILLE SCHOOL.** All cheer for me, Miss Gorgon, your new headmistress!"

The children in the hall gazed at her, open-mouthed in shock. This felt like a coup.

"I said cheer!" she demanded.

"Hooray!" cheered all the children.

All except Arthur.

"Now, straight after school, I want every single pupil, teacher and dinner lady at **BASKERVILLE SCHOOL** to assemble in the chapel. As it is my first day as head, I have a super surprise for you all!"

Arthur didn't like the sound of that, but, before he could ask another question, the bell rang for the first lesson of the day.

BRIIIING!

As all his classmates trudged off, shellshocked, to their triple Maths lesson, Arthur had other ideas. He needed to carry on with his investigation. So he slipped away from the other children, and tiptoed down the stone steps that led to the cellar. He wanted to see if whoever had done this to Mr Dust had left any **clues** behind.

Arthur's trusty paperclip did the trick. It was when he used it to pick the lock of the thick metal door to the cellar that he made his horrific discovery.

The huge, heavy door swung open.

CREAK!

The boy then stepped into the **darkness.**

With his torch guiding the way, Arthur found the stone figure of Mr Dust. From where it stood, right up against the corner of the cellar, Arthur deduced that Mr Dust had been **backing away** from whatever or whoever had done this to him.

He searched the floor for **clues,** his torch finding something lying near the **STATUE**. Bending down, Arthur realised that it was a glove.

A woman's glove.

A purple glove.

A glove he had seen before.

Just then he heard the sound of footsteps behind him.

CRUMP! CRUMP! CRUMP!

Instantly, he switched off the torch and stood still in the darkness. Arthur didn't dare breathe. He didn't want to make a sound. But whoever or whatever was down in the cellar with him was now breathing ice-cold air on his face.

SHIVER!

What would Sherlock do? thought Arthur.

He was sure the detective wouldn't have just tried to run away. Sherlock would have the courage to face his enemy!

"Who's th-th-there?" spluttered Arthur. He didn't sound quite as masterly as he had hoped.

"Your worst nightmare!" purred the figure lurking in the dark.

In terror, Arthur stumbled back. He hit the stone STATUE behind him hard.

THUMP!

So hard that his glasses fell off.

CLATTER!

Of course, he would know that voice in the dark anywhere. It was **Miss Gorgon!**

"MY GLASSES!" he cried.

"We need light for this to work!" she purred.

"For what to work?"

"You'll see!"

"I can't see!"

Miss Gorgon flicked a switch on the wall.

One bare light bulb, tangled in cobwebs, flickered on. It cast the cellar into a *whirling* dance of **SHADOWS.**

Arthur wasn't lying. He could barely see without his glasses.

However, this was never going to hold him back. It would prove to be his **_SUPERPOWER!_**

That's because Miss Gorgon pulled off her dark glasses to expose her piercing red eyes!

Then she took her silk handkerchief to her face and rubbed off the thick make-up. Underneath, her skin was green!

Finally, she threw off her hat to reveal that, instead of hair, she had a writhing mass of serpents – each one eviller than the last.

"HISS!"

"HISS!"

"HISS!"

The snakes didn't actually do anything. But they looked knockout. It wasn't clear, looking at them, if Miss Gorgon needed to use shampoo and a conditioner, but there wasn't time to think about that now.

"Who are you?" yelled Arthur, hearing the snakes but not seeing anything more than a green *blur* in front of him.

"I am not just plain Miss Gorgon!" she exclaimed. "I am a gorgon! My name is... Medusa!"

Arthur knew from all the History lessons that Medusa was a **TERRIFYING** figure from Ancient Greek legend. If you looked into her eyes, you would be turned to stone. For all eternity!

"NOO!" he cried, scrambling around the floor for his glasses. But just then he realised his glasses were the last thing he needed. If he looked at Medusa, he would become a stone **STATUE** too!

"Look into my eyes, Arthur! Meet your **DOOM!**" she purred.

"I have read all the books on ancient mythology! I thought Perseus had beheaded you!"

"No! I beheaded him! Don't believe everything you read!"

"What do you want?"

"To turn every last revolting child in this school to stone!"

"Why didn't you do that this morning?"

"It was only your year group, you foolish child! That is why I called a meeting of the entire school in the chapel this afternoon. Then I will fulfil my destiny!"

"You'll never do it!"

"Why is that, you pathetic little child detective?"

"Because this pathetic little child detective always comes prepared!"

Keeping his eyes tightly shut, Arthur scrabbled in his bag until he found his mirror. He pulled it out and held it up in Medusa's direction.

"ARGH!" she screamed until there was an *eerie* silence.

It was only when Arthur found his glasses on the floor that he could see what his quick thinking had achieved.

Medusa had turned to stone, a look of **FURY** etched on her face forever.

Looking in her own eyes in Arthur's little mirror had condemned her to the same fate as Mr Dust. Now there were two stone **STATUES** in the cellar.

"I wonder who will be in charge of **BASKERVILLE SCHOOL** now?" mused Arthur.

*

That afternoon, after the bell sounded at the end of the final lesson of the day, everyone headed for the chapel. Aside from Arthur, no one knew the **mystery** of what had happened to not just Mr Dust but also Miss Gorgon.

Everyone in the pews of the vast church building was looking around and muttering to each other. They had all been called here by Miss Gorgon, but the new headmistress had failed to make an appearance.

All eyes turned to the chapel door as it opened.

CREAK!

There was a collective sigh of disappointment, as it wasn't the headmistress but a bespectacled little boy wearing a deerstalker hat and a tweed cape. With the authority of Sherlock Holmes himself, he waltzed to the front of the chapel. There were some sniggers from the

bullies, and murmurs of nasty names like "noob". But with the quiet dignity of a master detective Arthur ignored them.

"School!" began the boy. "I have some not-so-sad news. I know many of you may be wondering where Miss Gorgon is. I'm pleased to inform you that our new headmistress has been taken rather ill. So ill, in fact, that she is dead! In a rather fortunate accident! With a mirror! Unfortunately for her, she looked into it!"

There was proper laughter now.

"HA! HA! HA!"

"So, for now at least, I, Arthur Doyle, am the new head of **BASKERVILLE SCHOOL!**"

There were murmurs of disapproval now, especially from the teachers.

"HOW DARE HE!"

"GIVE THAT BOY A DETENTION!"

"EXPEL HIM!"

"WAIT!" cried Arthur. "I have some new school rules! All chocolate bars in the tuck shop are now free!"

"HOORAY!" cheered the children.

"Because of the deep snow outside, the cross-country run is cancelled!"

"HOORAY!"

"Not just this year but every year!"

An even bigger "HOORAY!"

"And, finally, triple Maths is forbidden!"

"HOORAY!"

This was the biggest one yet.

"Instead, I am going to read to you my brand-new story. It's called 'The Curious Case of Miss Gorgon'!"

The boy cleared his throat.

"HUH-HUM!"

He began to read.

"The headmaster had been turned to stone!"

The chapel fell silent, as the entire school listened to the genius little detective.

FRANKENTEDDY

ONCE UPON A TIME, in a remote castle, lived
two children – a brother and sister named Percy
and Mary. He was nasty, but she was nice.
Percy was one of the world's worst children.
Oh, sorry, **wrong book.**

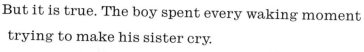

But it is true. The boy spent every waking moment trying to make his sister cry.

The castle was perched high on a cliff overlooking a **raging** sea. What made this castle special was that there was a secret laboratory hidden deep inside. The laboratory belonged to the children's father. His name was Dr Victor Frankenstein.

CUE THUNDER AND LIGHTNING...

BOOM!

CRACKLE!

FOLLOWED BY A STAB OF

DRAMATIC MUSIC...

DUM!

DUM!

DER!

Dr Frankenstein was a tall, thin man, with pale skin and dead eyes. It looked as if he hadn't slept in years. Which was true.

That was because he was a scientist who had a deep and dark obsession with bringing the dead back to life.

BOOM!

CRACKLE!

DUM! DUM! DER!

As a result, Frankenstein had been shunned by his fellow scientists. His **experiments** were considered deadly dangerous and deeply troubling. Frankenstein became infamous. However, that infamy just spurred him on. Day and night he toiled in his laboratory. He was a cold and **heartless** father; all he cared about was his work. Sometimes Frankenstein crept out of his castle in the dead of night and returned at dawn with sacks over his shoulder that dripped blood. Mary would see the red spots on the stone stairs leading down to the laboratory and wonder what on earth her wicked father was up to. She and her brother were forbidden to enter the laboratory.

One night, her curiosity got the better of her. Mary tiptoed down to the laboratory door and peeped through the keyhole. The girl could not believe what she saw. Her father was sewing together body parts he must have dug up from the graveyard. The man had made **A MONSTER!**

It was lying on a slab in the middle of the laboratory. A complex metal apparatus with **circles** and *wires* dangled overhead.

As he went about his work, Frankenstein babbled to himself. "I will become immortal! I will go down in history, not as a man, but as a god, because, as soon as lightning strikes, electricity will pass through the monster's body. And I, the great Victor Frankenstein, will achieve the impossible. I will bring the dead back to life!"

From that day on, Frankenstein would rarely emerge from his laboratory. When he did, he would climb the staircases to the very top of the castle and stand on one of the turrets. A huge kite attached to a metal wire flew overhead.

"Lightning! Strike!" Frankenstein would command.

But none came.

With his father so preoccupied with his deadly **experiment**, his son, Percy, was free to run riot. As their mother had long ago left the castle, the boy could unleash a reign of terror on his little sister.

Percy would...

...put live worms in Mary's slippers...

SQUIRM!

...place a huge block of ice at the bottom of her bed...

CHATTER!

...tell her nightmarish ghost stories right before bedtime...

"NOOOO! STOP!"

...squash moths in between the pages of her precious fairy-story books...

THWUCK!

...dress up in a medieval tunic, stick on a false beard and hide behind an empty picture frame, pretending to be a painting. When his unsuspecting sister walked past, he'd shout, "BOO!"...

"ARGH!"

...hide spiders in her morning porridge...

KERUNCH!

...fill her bath with eels...

YUCK!

...place owl eggs in her hair when she slept. Her hair became a nest. So, when Mary woke up, she had a family of owls living on her head...

HOOT! HOOT! HOOT!

...serve her toad-in-the-hole for dinner. But instead of there being a sausage in the batter there was a real-life toad...

RIBBIT!

And once he sneaked into Mary's bedroom while she was sleeping and snatched her precious teddy bear. Next, he took a gigantic pair of scissors and chopped it into pieces.

CHOP!

CHOP!

CHOP!

Then, armed with a spade, Percy buried the parts of the bear all over the grounds of the castle.

DIG!

DIG!

DIG!

I am sure you will agree that Percy was a monster. But the boy is not the monster of this story.

Oh no.

Come with me as we journey into the nightmare world of **THE MONSTER TEDDY BEAR!**

Now, Mary loved her teddy like no child had ever loved a teddy before. Her life in the castle was desperately lonely. Byron the bear was her one and only friend. It didn't matter that he couldn't move on his own, or talk,

or even smile. Mary loved every patch of fur on him. By day, she tucked him up safely in her four-poster bed. By night, she held him tight, cuddling him until dawn.

So when Mary woke up that morning she instantly noticed something was very wrong.

There was **no** Byron lying next to her.

She looked everywhere.

Beneath the sheets

Beside the pillows

Under the bed

But her precious teddy bear was nowhere to be found.

"BYRON!" she screamed.

The scream echoed all around the castle.

Outside the door, Percy was sniggering away at his latest trick.

"TEE! HEE! HEE!"

But that wicked grin was about to be wiped off his face... forever!

Mary was a feisty soul. She swung open her bedroom door and shouted, "PERCY! YOU VILE BRUTE! WHERE IS BYRON?"

Far down the corridor, she spotted her **dastardly** brother scurrying away. She ran after him, *leaped* into the air and tackled him to the ground.

184

THUMP!

Despite being smaller than Percy, she was stronger, and pinned him to the floor.

"Get off me!" cried the boy, rolling himself from side to side to escape her clutches.

"Not until you tell me where to find Byron!"

"I have no idea!" lied Percy.

"I don't believe you! TELL ME!"

"NEVER!"

Mary spotted that her brother's hands were black with dirt. She grabbed one and took a closer look. There was **soil** under his fingernails.

"YOU BURIED HIM, DIDN'T YOU?" she demanded.

"NO!"

Mary hated to resort to torture, but felt she had no choice. She twisted her brother's ears until they went bright red.

"ARGH! YES! YES! I DID!" he cried.

"You will pay for this!" warned Mary. "You will pay for this if it is the last thing I do!"

With that, she rose from the floor and marched off down the corridor.

She put on her boots and rushed out of the castle into the grounds. Dawn was breaking, and a wicked wind had *whipped* up from the sea. There were little mounds of earth all around. This must be where Byron was buried. Defiantly, Mary grabbed the spade lying on the ground nearby and, one by one, she dug up the remains.

Bits were buried everywhere...

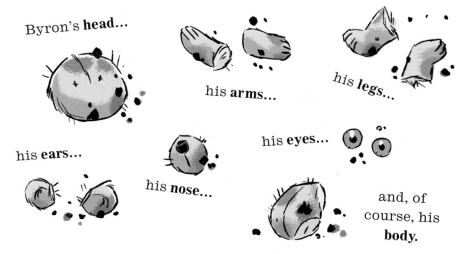

Byron's **head**...

his **arms**...

his **legs**...

his **ears**...

his **nose**...

his **eyes**...

and, of course, his **body.**

His fur was blackened from the **soil.**

It was dusk by the time Mary had found and dug up all the pieces of Byron.

She took them all up to her bedroom and attempted to sew him back together. However, the girl had no clue how to **sew.** With tears in her eyes, she sewed and sewed. Sadly, by the time she had finished, Byron looked **monstrous.**

Arms and legs were in the wrong places.

His head was sewn on back to front.

One of his eyes had gone missing.

His ears had been placed far too low.

His beautiful thick brown fur was damp, **dark** and **pongy.**

Byron looked like a

MONSTER!

"I am sorry. You look terrifying now, Byron!"

Then Mary had a thought. A wicked thought. So wicked it was **genius.**

"But you would give my brother a terrible **fright!**" she said to her bear. "If only I could attempt what my father is trying to do and bring you to **life.** Now that would be seriously scary!"

Just then she heard a r u m b l e of thunder outside her window.

BOOM!

A storm was breaking. Lightning was sure to strike.

Mary dashed down to the depths of the castle, clutching her bear. She hid in the shadows until her father scurried out of his laboratory and raced up the stone steps.

As he did so, Mary slipped inside. Immediately, she shivered. The laboratory was spooktastic!*

Chemicals BuBBLED away in test tubes. A huge blackboard with hundreds of mathematical equations scribbled in chalk hung on the wall. All around the laboratory, body parts floated in jars.

A brain. A heart. A hand. Eyeballs. A foot. Even a buttock!

* A real word you will find in your Walliamsictionary.

The monster was still laid out on the slab, motionless.

Mary tiptoed over to take a closer look. It had a swollen head, green skin and **ODD** hands and feet sewn on it. It was **monstrous!** Which is just as well, as it was a monster!

Either side of the monster's temples were two metal discs. These discs were connected by wires to the metal rings overhead.

"These must be to bring the monster to life!" she said to herself.

Quickly, she detached them from the monster and put them on to her teddy bear's head instead.

CRACKLE!

Lightning had at last struck.

But nothing happened.

Looking up at the apparatus, Mary noticed that a wire had come loose.

"Father must have missed this!" she whispered to herself.

She climbed up on to the slab and put the end of the wire in what looked like the right place.

Mary removed her hand just in time as...

CRACKLE!

...a bolt of **lightning** must have finally struck the kite, because the rings lit up, sparks flew from the **wire** and the metal discs **glowed**.

Then the impossible happened.

The monster teddy

blinked its eye.

It was alive!

The thing stood perfectly **upright,** before looking at her.

Hastily, Mary placed the metal discs **back** on the monster's head. If her father found out she had ventured into his laboratory, he would punish her like never before.

Next, Mary grabbed her monster teddy and darted out of the laboratory.

Hearing her father's footsteps echoing along the corridor, Mary hid in the shadows until he passed. He slammed the door behind him.

SHUNT!

Outside the castle, the storm raged.

Thunder.

BOOM!

Lightning. CRACKLE!

"Monster Teddy!" said Mary, placing him down on the ground. "I command you to go to my brother Percy's bedroom and give him the fright of his life!"

The thing nodded its head and they climbed the staircases to the bedroom floor. Soon, they had reached Percy's door.

Not tall enough to reach the handle, the monster teddy looked at Mary, who gently opened the door.

CREAK!

It was now the dead of night. Despite the noise of the

thunder, the boy was fast asleep in his bed, snoring loudly.

"ZzZ! ZzZZ! zZZzZ!"

The monster teddy **marched** in.

Mary watched from the door, smirking, as it climbed up on to the boy's four-poster bed. It tiptoed over the blanket until it had reached Percy.

The monster teddy sat on top of the boy's head and lifted one of its arms.

It brought the arm down at speed, biffing him super-hard on the nose.

THWACK!

Percy let out a scream of pain.

"ARGH!"

His eyes opened to see this monster looming over him.

"GRRR!" growled the monster teddy.

"NOOOO!"

cried the boy.

He sat bolt upright in bed before trying to **yank** the thing off his head.

However, the monster teddy had gripped on with its legs, and was now boxing Percy's ears with its paws.

POW! **POW!** **POW!**

"OW!" "OW!" "OW!"

"HA! HA! HA!" laughed Mary.

Percy saw his little sister looking on from the doorway.

"MAKE IT STOP!" he pleaded.

"NEVER!" she replied.

Percy leaped out of bed and began running down the stairs, all the time trying to **wrestle** the monster teddy off his head.

"GET OFF ME!"

But the thing had super-strength, and it was impossible.

Another bolt of lightning struck.

CRACKLE!

"FATHER!" cried Percy. "HELP ME!"

As the monster teddy poked Percy in the eye, the boy bolted down towards his father's laboratory. Mary chased after them.

However, as they descended into the darkness, they heard a deafening roar.

"ROAR!"

They stopped at the top of the steps that led down to the laboratory.

Out of the gloom stepped their father. A wicked grin was painted on his face.

"Children!" he began. "I want you to meet my masterpiece! Your genius father has made the dead live again! Behold the greatest creation in the history of the world! FRANKENSTEIN'S MONSTER!"

Out of the shadows lumbered a figure. It took its place by its creator's side, dwarfing the doctor.

This was a **colossus** of a creature. The monster to end all monsters!

"ROAR!"

Percy and Mary trembled with fear.

"F-F-Father. Wh-wh-what have you done?" spluttered Mary.

"The impossible!" he replied.

The only one who wasn't scared was the monster teddy. To Percy's relief, it slid off the boy's head all the way to the floor.

"What devilment is this?" demanded Father.

"Oh!" replied Mary. "I forgot to mention! I achieved the impossible too. I brought my teddy bear back to life!"

"But you are a mere child!"

"Still got there first, Pops!"

The monster teddy marched over to Frankenstein's monster.

"ROAR!" roared the big monster at the little monster.

But the monster teddy wasn't the least bit frightened.

"GRRRRR!" growled the little monster.

The big monster scooped it up into its hands.

"DON'T DESTROY IT!" cried Mary.

Her father flashed a sinister smile. "It will be ripped to shreds, you silly little fool!"

"I was talking to my teddy!"

"WHAT?"

"You'll see!"

Percy nodded his head in agreement.

Sadly for the big monster, the little monster did not obey its creator's command. Instead, it **bit** into the big monster's giant finger.

"AAARRRGHHH!"

screamed the big monster.

Instantly, it dropped the teddy, who then kicked the big monster. **Hard.**

"YOWEE!" it yelped, clutching itself.

It doubled over in pain before pushing past the children to the front door of the castle. Instead of opening the door, it burst right through it.

CRASH!

The Frankenstein family and the little monster dashed to the doorway to watch it go. The little monster had the smuggest smile on its furry face.

The big monster fled as fast as it could. It stumbled and fell.

"OOF!"

It then began rolling down the hill like a giant ball.

As it rolled faster and faster,

it broke up into pieces.

The great Dr Victor Frankenstein must have been even worse at sewing than his daughter.

First the monster's head snapped off.

Then an arm.

Then a leg.

Then another arm.

Then its other leg.

All the pieces then rolled off the cliff and landed in the freezing sea below.

PLOP! PLOP! PLOP! PLOP!

They bobbed in the water, carried away by the tide.

WHOOSH!

"NOOO!" cried Frankenstein. "MY LIFE'S WORK! DESTROYED FOREVER!"

"Oops!" remarked Mary with a smirk.

"You will pay for this, Mary! Your little life will not be worth living!"

"Mmm," mused Mary. "I think not. Monster teddy is in charge now!"

Her little monster stepped over to her, and she scooped it up into her arms.

"**GRRRR!**" it growled at Dr Frankenstein.

The man was so **terrified** he hid behind his son.

"P-p-please don't hurt me!" he pleaded.

But the teddy marched round and booted the man in the bottom.

Dr Frankenstein burst into tears…

"BOO! HOO! HOO!"

…as his daughter burst into laughter.

"HA! HA! HA!"

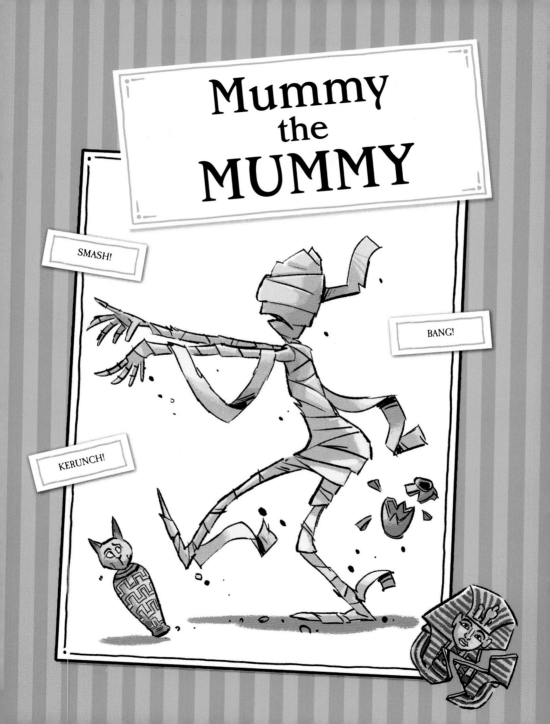

Mummy
the
MUMMY

When is a mummy not a mummy? When the mummy is, in fact, a mummy.

Please indulge me for one moment.

Let's begin this **HORROR** story with a history lesson.

This is a

mummy...

...an Ancient Egyptian who, after death, had been mummified to prepare them for the afterlife.

The priests of the time would remove all the insides except the heart, embalm the body to preserve it, then wrap it from head to toe in strips of linen until it was completely covered.

These mummies were discovered thousands of years later by archaeologists, who found their tombs buried deep under the sand in the deserts of Egypt. *Legend* has it that disturbing these burial sites causes ancient curses to be unleashed. Many of the archaeologists died in **mysterious** circumstances. Some even believed that if you unearthed these mummies they came back to life as monsters!

Now, this is also a mummy:

This is Jess's mummy. Jess is a little girl in glasses who loves her mummy, even though she is the clumsiest person on earth.

Jess's mummy was a lovely lady who wore brightly coloured dresses and big flowery hats. This was just as well, as you could see her coming from a mile away. Every time she had a mishap, she said, "WHOOPSIES!"

Mummy was a one-woman disaster zone:

Stepping inside the house from a rainstorm, Mummy closed her umbrella on her head. She couldn't see a thing.

SNUTCH!

"WHOOPSIES!"

Mummy stumbled through the house and into the back garden. There, she stepped into the pond.

SPLOOSH!

"WHOOPSIES!"

Impatiently waiting for a piece of toast to pop out of a toaster, Mummy found herself peering in. The piece of toast shot UP and whacked her on the nose.

BONK!

"WHOOPSIES!"

Shoving a heavy book on to the wrong shelf at the library, Mummy set off a chain reaction. Every single book *toppled* over like dominoes, burying her under a mountain of books.

THUNK!
"WHOOPSIES!"

Repairing a vase that she had broken, Mummy managed to superglue her dress to the table without realising. **GLOOP!**

When she stood up and walked away, her dress stayed stuck to the table.

RIP!

Mummy stood there in her undercrackers.

"WHOOPSIES!"

Once Mummy got her shampoo bottle and her tomato-ketchup bottles mixed up. So she ate some shampoo-flavoured chips...

"YUCK!"

...and her hair turned bright red.

"WHOOPSIES!"

Placing a box of cereal in her supermarket trolley, Mummy toppled in.

PLUNK!

The force of her fall sent the trolley speeding down the aisle.

WHIZZ!

It knocked over shoppers as it zoomed.

BOINK! BOINK! BOINK!

All the time, Mummy's legs waggled in the air.

"WHOOPSIES!"

Mummy mistook her slice of chocolate cake for the telephone. When she heard a **ring,** she pushed the cake to her ear instead.

SQUELCH!

"WHOOPSIES!"

A year later, Mummy was still finding cake crumbs in her ear. Still, it made for a handy snack while riding the bus, much to the horror of her fellow passengers.

Leaning over the safety barrier too far at the zoo, Mummy plunged into the penguin pool. The poor lady couldn't hoist herself out of the water. Mummy ended up splashing around in there for the best part of a year, surviving only on a diet of raw fish.

SQUAWK! SQUAWK! SQUAWK! "WHOOPSIES!"

Her daughter Jess couldn't be more different from her. She was a shy, studious girl who had been learning about

Ancient Egypt in school. Everything about the subject **electrified** her:

The gold death masks

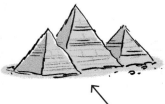

The Sphinx

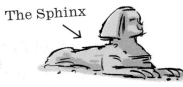

The pyramids

The River Nile

The tombs

The Valley of the Kings

The invention of toothpaste. And clocks! And calendars! And paper! And ink! And police!

The more than 700 symbols of hieroglyphs (or ancient writing with pictures)

The sagas of the royal families and pharaohs

That everyone wore make-up

The female pharaoh Hatshepsut who wore a fake beard!

The 2,000 and more gods and goddesses they worshipped

The bathing in sour milk

The fact that Ancient Egyptians believed that cats were sacred and often mummified them too!

However, at the top of Jess's list were, of course, the mummies. She even had fantastical dreams about the curses. Jess imagined these mummies coming back to life to wreak revenge on those who had disturbed their final resting place. She was absolutely fascinated by them and longed to see one in real life.

So, on the eve of her **birthday,** Jess pleaded, "Mummy, please, please, please can you take me to the British Museum for my **birthday** so I can see the mummies with my own eyes?"

"Darling, please, no! Those things give Mummy the willies!" replied her mother, putting down her book, which was upside down.

"Please?"

"No! Can't we go to the circus instead?"

"The last time we went to the circus, Mummy, you got tangled in the high-wire act and ended up smashing into the side of the tent and bringing the entire thing crashing to the ground."

"A minor mishap," chirped Mummy. "I know! How about we visit the fair?"

"Our last trip to the fair was an even greater catastrophe!"

"I haven't the foggiest as to what you are talking about, Jessica."

Jess rolled her eyes. "Have you forgotten what happened on the **bumper** cars?"

Mummy shrugged.

"You went far too fast, **smashed** through the barrier and crashed into the big wheel, knocking it off its axis!" continued Jess.

"Well, I'm sure some of those people enjoyed having a *free roll* across the park. They were screaming *with delight!*"

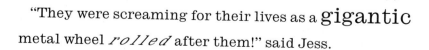

"They were screaming for their lives as a gigantic metal wheel *rolled* after them!" said Jess.

"I know! Let's go to the **waterslides!**"

Jess couldn't believe her ears. "Mummy, you have a lifetime ban from the **waterslides!**"

"Do I?" asked Mummy, trying to sound innocent.

"Yes! You tried to go up the

waterslides rather than

down

them!"

"How was I meant to know?"

"A dozen people were rushed to hospital that day. Including you!"

"All I did was break every bone in my body. A lot of fuss about nothing, if you ask me!"

"HUMPH!" huffed Jess. "It's my **birthday** and I want to go to the British Museum. But you must promise me, Mummy, to be on your absolute best behaviour. No more disasters!"

"As if!"

"MUMMY!"

"I PROMISE!" replied Mummy with a big, broad smile. One that Jess couldn't share.

So, the very next morning, mother and daughter set off on the train to the museum.

It was still early, but Mummy had already managed to...

...sit on her daughter's **birthday** cake, resulting in it sticking to her bottom...

SQUELCH!

"WHOOPSIES!"

...accidentally cover Muddles the family dog in wrapping paper instead of Jess's present...

"WHOOPSIES!" RUSTLE!

...and sing **"Happy Birthday"** in such a high voice that all the windows in the house cracked...

CRACK! "WHOOPSIES!"

Despite all this, Jess was sure that a trip to the British Museum was going to make today the best **birthday** ever. Little did she know the *whirlwind* of chaos and destruction her mummy was about to unleash on the world.

As soon as the pair arrived at the grand building, Mummy announced she needed the loo.

"It's just there," said Jess, pointing to a door. "I'll be in the mummy room."

"Of course, dear," replied Mummy, scuttling off to the ladies'.

Stepping into the mummy room, Jess was struck silent with awe. All around the room were ORNATE coffins standing upright. Each one contained an Ancient Egyptian mummy.

Next to these coffins were treasures from their tombs that they believed they would need in the afterlife.

Now, Mummy had a bad habit of using up **all** the toilet paper in the house. That is because she always tugged too hard on the end of the roll, and the entire thing would *unspool.*

This is precisely what she did in the museum toilet cubicle. Mummy yanked on the end and the bumper-size roll began *unspooling* at speed.

WHIRR!

"WHOOPSIES!"

In her futile attempts to roll the paper back into place, Mummy managed to tangle herself up in it. The more she **struggled,** the worse it became. Soon she was covered from **head** to **toe** in toilet paper.

BEFORE

AFTER

Mummy now looked exactly like a mummy!

As she stumbled out of the cubicle with her arms outstretched, the ladies at the basins screamed in horror.

"A MUMMY!" "ARGH!"

"HELP!"

Mummy the mummy tried to speak, but her words were **muffled** by the toilet paper stuck in her mouth. All you could hear were scary-sounding moans.

"URGH!"

Mummy's eyes were completely covered so she couldn't see where she was going. She stumbled into the museum, grabbing visitors and holding on to them tightly for fear of falling over. The poor souls wriggled out of her grip and ran for their lives.

"NOOO!" "IT'S ALIVE!"

"THE MUMMY WILL KILL US ALL!"

Now Mummy the mummy was **LUMBERING** along the corridor of the museum in the direction of the mummy room where the mummies were.*

As Mummy stumbled forward, she **bumped** into marble statues of emperors, toppling them to the ground.

* I just broke the world record for the most times "mummy" is used in a sentence.

KERUNCH!

She swept priceless Roman vases off their shelves with her outstretched arms.

SMASH! CRASH! BANG!

And even staggered into a security guard.

BOOF!

The man had been enjoying a crafty snooze in his chair, but now woke up to find a mummy crashing into him.

"URGH!" moaned Mummy the mummy.

"AAAHHH!" cried the security guard as he fled down the corridor, tears streaming down his face.

Jess was completely immersed in the ancient world of wonder when the bandaged figure **shuffled** into the room behind her. As all the other visitors around her ran off, she felt a tap on her shoulder. She turned round slowly to see this mummy – well, her mummy... well, her mummy dressed as a mummy, who of course she thought was a mummy, despite it being her mummy, behind her.*

"ARGH!" screamed the girl.

"URGH!" moaned Mummy the mummy.

"It's true! There is a curse!"

Jess picked up the nearest weapon she could find, a leaflet on Ancient Egypt, and brandished it in the direction of the mummy.

"Don't come any closer or I will be forced to POKE you repeatedly with this leaflet!"

Tripping up on the toilet paper wrapped around her shoes, Mummy the mummy stumbled forward.

"URGH!"

"I did warn you!" exclaimed Jess. She tried to POKE the mummy with the leaflet, but all that happened was that the paper bent.

CRUNKLE!

---

* A NEW WORLD RECORD! And don't try to top it by just writing "mummy mummy mummy mummy mummy mummy mummy"! That is not a proper sentence.

"Oh!" murmured the girl. But then she had a better idea. She grabbed hold of the end of what she assumed was linen (but was of course bog roll) and yanked hard.

YUNK!

"TAKE THAT, MUMMY!" she cried.

In an instant, Mummy the mummy began *spinning* wildly.

WHIZZ!

As the toilet paper *twirled* off, she whirled around the room, colliding with the ancient coffins holding the real mummies.

THUNK! THUNK! THUNK!

One by one, the coffins toppled off their plinths and crashed to the ground.

SMASH! SMASH! SMASH!

Even the little coffin containing the mummified cat broke.

⸗ SMISH! ⸗

Shards and splinters of wood were scattered across the floor. Now all the mummies had been well and truly woken from their eternal sleeps. The mummified cat also began to stir.

"MIAOW!"

With the roll of toilet paper now unfurled on the museum floor, Mummy was finally free, if more than a little **dizzy.**

"MUMMY!" exclaimed Jess. "I thought you were a real mummy come to life!"

"Oh no!" chuckled her mother. "I just had a fight with a roll of toilet paper!"

Jess rushed over to Mummy and gave her the biggest hug.

"Oh! I am so relieved!" she sighed.

What Mummy could see, but her daughter could not, was that the real mummies lying on the floor of the museum were twitching into life.

"Erm, Jessica..."

"Yes!"

"Don't be too relieved, because I think your mummy has made another **boo-boo.**

WHOOPSIES!

Double WHOOPSIES!

And triple WHOOPSIES!"

Jess spun round. She couldn't believe what she saw.
A dozen ancient mummies were rising to their feet
and stumbling towards them with their hands
outstretched. Even the mummified cat was approaching.

"HISS!"

"WHOOPSIES!" said Mummy.

The mummies began trying to grab at the pair.

"URGH!" they moaned.

IT WAS TERRIFYING!

From under the bandages, their eyes shone **red** like demons.

GLOW!

"NO!" screamed Jess as a mummified hand gripped on to her arm. "GET OFF ME!"

"What shall we do?" cried Mummy, who had a mummified hand on her shoulder.

"Let me think!"

Jess was smart, and her brain PINGED with an idea so clever even she was shocked by her own genius.

"I KNOW! Grab one end of the toilet roll, and I will grab the other!"

"Righty-ho!" said Mummy. "Then what?"

"Wrap them all up in it!"

That is exactly what they did.

The pair each took an end of the roll and ran around the museum in huge circles, wrapping the mummies in paper so they couldn't come any closer.

The mummified cat was clever, though, and it ducked out of the way and hid behind a statue.

Meanwhile, the mummies were bound up together. They couldn't move a millimetre.

"URGH!"

"Such a clever girl!" said Mummy.

"I know!" joked Jess.

At that moment, some security guards who were braver than the crying one came bursting into the room.

"WHOOPSIES! Time to leave!" whispered Mummy.

She took her daughter's hand and they slunk out of the museum, not even stopping at the gift shop. The gift shop, as we all know, is always the best part of any museum. Where else would you buy a vastly overpriced eraser?

YES! Things were that serious!

It was only when Jess was being tucked into bed that night that she remembered something.

"The cat!"

"The what?" asked Mummy.

"The mummified cat! In the museum. It came back to life, but we didn't wrap it in toilet roll!"

"I am sure the security guards have found it."

"I do hope so," replied Jess, her brow wrinkled with worry.

"So, Jessica, did you have a lovely **birthday?**"

"Well, apart from you being wrapped head to toe in a roll of toilet paper, destroying most of the precious artefacts in the museum and bringing some Ancient Egyptian mummies back to life, yes!"

Mummy smiled. "WHOOPSY DOOPSY DOO!"

She bent down to kiss her daughter on the head, but slipped on Jess's slipper and fell on top of her instead.

"OOF!" exclaimed Jess.

"WHOOPSIES! I am so sorry, darling!"

"Don't worry, Mummy. I love you! And I always will!"

"I love you too! *Sweet dreams*, my beautiful angel!"

Mummy then managed to trip over Jess's other slipper and fell headfirst into the light switch.

DUMPH!

"WHOOPSIES!"

The force of the blow turned the light off. As Mummy closed the door, she trapped her nightdress inside...

RIP!

...ripping the whole thing off.

"WHOOPSIES!" came a voice from the other side of the door. "Not again! I'm all in the nudey nudes!"

Her daughter couldn't help but burst into laughter.

"HA! HA! HA!"

She felt so lucky having the **funniest** mummy in the world. Tired, Jess rolled over on to her side to sleep. Just as her eyes flickered shut, she heard a gentle tapping on the window.

TAP! TAP! TAP!

Jess slid out of bed and tiptoed over to investigate. Peeping through the gap in the curtains, she could see **something** perched on the ledge.

It was the mummified cat from the museum, its eyes glowing **red** like a demon.

"WHOOPSIES!" whispered Jess.

This was **no** nightmare!

This was **really** happening!

"HISS!"

The ABOMINABLE
but ∧ Nice SNOWMAN

ABOM

IN

ABLE

The ABOMINABLE
but Nice SNOWMAN

LORD BLUNDERBUSS thought himself an explorer, **adventurer** and hunter. That meant he liked to go abroad and shoot things.

He looked like this:

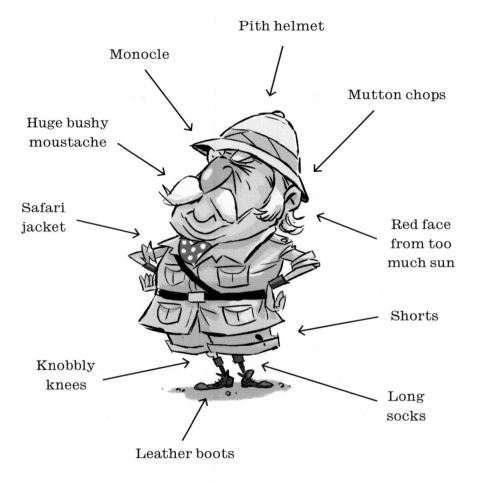

Pith helmet

Monocle

Mutton chops

Huge bushy moustache

Safari jacket

Red face from too much sun

Shorts

Knobbly knees

Long socks

Leather boots

It was the 1920s when this tale began. Lord Blunderbuss was slumped in his leather armchair in his grand old country house, **BLUNDERBUSS MANOR.** He was surrounded by hundreds of stuffed animals he'd hunted over his lifetime.

Now they stood in dramatic poses all around **BLUNDERBUSS MANOR**. In every corner of the house there were:

Hippopotamuses

Orang-utans

Jellyfish

Elephants

Crocodiles

Lions

Wasps

Giraffes

Polar bears

Tigers

Gorillas

It was a scene of horror for any animal lovers, but a source of great **pride** to Lord Blunderbuss. The hunter thought of himself as terribly brave for having hunted all these animals, even though he was the one armed with a gun, not them. And they were running away at the time. He even shot a flea. It took hundreds of goes to hit the poor thing.

Now, with nothing left to shoot, Blunderbuss was bored. Bored out of his tiny brain.

"NANNY!" he shouted.

Despite being in his sixties, Blunderbuss was still looked after by his childhood nanny. She was not his grandmother but a lady his parents had employed to care for him since he was a baby.

"Yes, your lordship?" she replied, shuffling into the study, an ear trumpet held to her head.

"Nanny, I am so bored. I have shot every known creature on the planet. I have nothing to shoot next!"

"Perhaps it's time to hang up your rifle for good, your lordship!" she suggested.

"NEVER!" he thundered. "Would you mind awfully if I shot you?"

"I would really rather you didn't," replied the old lady.

"Yes. Who would bring me my tea and scones?" he reasoned.

"Exactly! Of course, there are legendary beasts, your lordship."

"What exactly do you mean?"

"Creatures that no one knows for sure really exist."

"Like a rhinoceros made entirely of cheese? A PIANO-PLAYING turtle? A camel that speaks Japanese?"

"No! Like a unicorn, or a dragon, or a mermaid, or a griffin, or a sea serpent."

 "FETCH ME MY RIFLE!" he bellowed.
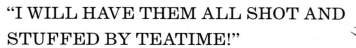 "I WILL HAVE THEM ALL SHOT AND 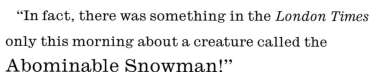 STUFFED BY TEATIME!"

"In fact, there was something in the *London Times* only this morning about a creature called the Abominable Snowman!"

"Sounds abominable!"

Nanny rolled her eyes. "That it does! It was spotted on an expedition to Mount Everest!"

"Hand me the newspaper!"

"It's right there next to you, your lordship," replied Nanny.

Indeed it was – on top of a pile of newspapers on a coffee table right next to his armchair. It couldn't be nearer.

"Don't be so impudent, Nanny! Hand it to me!"

The old lady shuffled over to Lord Blunderbuss and passed the newspaper to him.

"LAZY OAF!" he shouted into her ear trumpet. "Now, I am exhausted from all this sitting down and scoffing biscuits – you read it to me!"

Nanny cleared her throat and began: "This morning at the top of the Himalayan mountains there was a sighting of a huge, ape-like creature with white fur and large, sharp teeth! It has been named the Abominable Snowman!"

"Sounds ideal for a good old-fashioned shooting and stuffing! We leave at dawn!"

"We?" asked Nanny. "I think I'm growing too old for all this travelling."

"Nonsense, Nanny! You don't look a day over eighty!"

"I am seventy-nine!"

"Well, there you are! And I need someone to carry all the bags!"

Nanny sighed to herself. "HUH!"

She had endured a **lifetime** of this.

*

The next morning at dawn, Nanny was standing at the front door of **BLUNDERBUSS MANOR** holding dozens of bags, trunks and suitcases. SO many, in fact, that Nanny was barely visible.

"NANNY! WHERE THE BLAZES ARE YOU?" demanded Blunderbuss.

"I am under here!"

came a voice.

"UNDER WHERE?"

"Under all your bags."

"Oh, Nanny! For goodness' sake, let me help you!" announced Lord Blunderbuss.

"Why thank you, your lordship!" she chirped.

He reached into the forest of luggage and took the umbrella she'd been holding between her teeth and marched outside.

"COME ALONG, NANNY! NO DAWDLING!" he called over his shoulder.

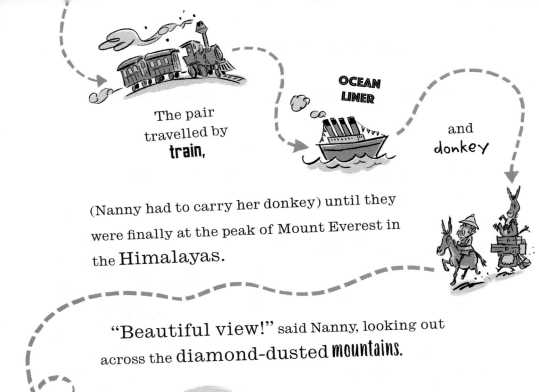

The pair travelled by **train,** OCEAN LINER and donkey

(Nanny had to carry her donkey) until they were finally at the peak of Mount Everest in the Himalayas.

"Beautiful view!" said Nanny, looking out across the diamond-dusted mountains.

"That is kind of you to say," replied Lord Blunderbuss, **twirling** his moustache. "I know I am looking ridiculously handsome today! Now, where is this Abominable Snowman?"

Nanny looked down and spotted large **FOOTPRINTS** in the snow.

"These could be the beast's!" she exclaimed.

Lord Blunderbuss bent down and examined them.

"I am a genius, Nanny!" he announced.

"I have found the Abominable Snowman's **FOOTPRINTS!** Follow me!"

Nanny stumbled through the snow and ice after him.

They passed a sign that read:

DANGER! *AVALANCHE!*

Blunderbuss being Blunderbuss read it out loud in his **booming** voice.

"DANGER! *AVALANCHE!*"

"SHUSH!" shushed Nanny. "You might set one off!"

"BALDERDASH!" he thundered.

The trail of the monster's **FOOTPRINTS** stretched for miles. It looped all around the Himalayas. Then there was an abrupt change of direction as it headed down the mountain to the forest below.

Nanny put a telescope to her eye and spotted a **shape**

stalking through the trees. It looked like a giant ape sporting a white fur coat. The monster stood on two legs, had piercing red eyes, and teeth so sharp they would give you **NIGHTMARES.** The Abominable Snowman must be hunting for food. He found some yellow snow and ate that.

"BLEURGH!" The monster spat it out.

"Can you see this abominable chap?" demanded Lord Blunderbuss.

"NO!" lied Nanny.

"Give me that telescope!" he thundered, snatching it out of her hands. "THERE IT IS! Hand me my rifle!"

"Let me just load it for you, your lordship!"

She reached into her pocket and pulled out some special bullets. Slowly, she placed them in the gun.

"For goodness' sake, hurry up!" he bellowed.

Blunderbuss snatched the rifle from her and took aim. As he did so, Nanny pretended to stumble and began sliding down the **mountain** on one of the luggage trunks.

The **mountain** was steep and slippery, and she sped down it at spectacular speed.

WHOOSH!

"Out of the way, Nanny!" bellowed Blunderbuss, shooting warning shots into the air.

BANG! BANG! BANG!

There followed the sound of a deep rumble like thunder.

BOOM!

Then snow and ice began *tumbling* from the peaks. **KERUNCH!**

It swept Blunderbuss off his feet!

"BOTHER!"

he shouted.

Nanny was travelling faster than the **AVALANCHE.**
Because of her head start, she made it to the trees before
the tidal wave of snow.

However, because Nanny was sliding on a trunk, she
couldn't control **where** she was going.

246

The heavy trunk struck the Abominable Snowman.

HARD! SHONT!

The monster *whizzed* through the air...

WHOOSH!

...landing right on top of Nanny.

BOOF!

"URGH!" she cried.

"ARGH!" the monster exclaimed on seeing an old lady.

Meanwhile, Lord Blunderbuss was tumbling down the **mountain** inside a giant snowball.

WHIRR!

"HELP!" he cried.

"Who are you?" demanded the Abominable Snowman.

"You can talk!" exclaimed Nanny.

"Yes, of course I can talk!"

"I didn't know the Abominable Snowman could talk!"

"Is that what they call me? Abominable? The cheek! I am **nice**, really!"

"I just saw you eat some yellow snow. That is pretty abominable."

"I thought it was **lemon-flavoured** snow – how wrong I was! The white snow gets very samey."

"Whatever you do, don't try the brown snow," warned Nanny.

"I did yesterday. I thought it was **chocolate-flavoured** snow." Nanny pulled a disgusted face.

RUMBLE!

The **AVALANCHE** had now reached the forest, but the trees slowed it down to a stop.

The giant snowball in which Blunderbuss was encased struck a boulder.

THUMP!

It **cracked** open like an egg, and a dazed and confused Blunderbuss fell out, still clinging on to his rifle.

"Who's that?" asked the monster.

"It's my boss, Lord Blunderbuss."

"Oh! I've never met a lord! Is he nice?"

"No. He's come to shoot you!"

"WHAT?" cried the monster, his eyes filling with tears. "I am too pretty to die!"

"Listen! Do exactly as I say, and you will be all right! For years he has been hunting animals all over the world, but instead of real bullets I have always loaded

his rifle with blanks. They make the same bang, but nothing shoots out. All you have to do is fall to the ground when you hear a bang and keep very still."

"All seems rather involved!"

"Do you want to live?" asked Nanny.

"I would prefer to."

"Then you need to play dead!"

Not far away, there was the sound of footsteps in the snow.

"Get ready!" whispered Nanny.

The Abominable Snowman stood up and tried to lean as casually as he could against a tree.

"MORNING!" he chirped.

"I'VE GOT YOU NOW, MONSTER!" cried Blunderbuss.

He brought the rifle up to his chest, but before he pulled the trigger the Abominable Snowman pretended to be hit in the chest.

"OW! I'VE BEEN HIT!" he cried. "OH, WOE! OH, WOE! OH, THRICE WOE!"

There followed an elaborate and dramatic performance of being in the throes of death.

"ARGH! URGH! NO!"

"He hasn't pulled the trigger yet!" whispered Nanny.

"OOPS!"

Then there was a deafening **BANG!**

This time the Abominable Snowman did nothing. Of course, it was a blank.

"NOW!" called out Nanny. "Pretend he's shot you! And less of the *theatrics*!"

The monster then performed an elegant *dive* on to the forest floor.

SLUMP!

"Is the monster dead?" cried Blunderbuss from a few paces away.

Nanny shuffled over to the Abominable Snowman.

"Yes!" she lied. "Well done, Lord Blunderbuss! So brave of you!"

"It was as if the bullet struck the beast before I even pulled the trigger."

"Well, that just proves what an expert marksman you are!"

"Does it?" he asked, bemused.

"YES! You are a hero! Now, let's get this latest trophy of yours back to **BLUNDERBUSS MANOR** and stuff it!"

"You never said anything about stuffing?" whispered the Abominable Snowman.

"SHUSH!" shushed Nanny.

The three travelled by donkey, **BOAT** and train.

All the time, poor Nanny had to carry the Abominable Snowman on her shoulders. And, of course, her donkey, who was

heavy!

The trouble started as soon as they entered through the front door of **BLUNDERBUSS MANOR.**

All the animals that Lord Blunderbuss thought he had shot and killed, and that he had assigned Nanny to stuff, were very much alive. They had just become experts at keeping still when Lord Blunderbuss was in the same room. All the rest of the time, they roamed the house and grounds. When Blunderbuss was off on his hunting trips, they even invited other animals over for drinks and nibbles.

However, none of them had ever seen an Abominable Snowman before. So, when Nanny staggered in carrying the furry monster on her shoulders, all the animals stopped standing still and went **BANANAS!**

They charged all around the house, knocking everything over. It was mayhem!

"ROO!" "RUFF!" "HISS!" "WHOOP!" "HONK!"

It was like a zoo! Well, it was a zoo!

"ARGH!" screamed Blunderbuss in terror, swept off his feet by wild beasts. "THE ANIMALS!

THEY'VE ALL COME BACK TO LIFE!"

"What are the chances of that?" chirped Nanny as an elephant charged past.

"HELP ME, NANNY! HELP ME!" he shouted from a silk rug as a tiger began playing with him with its paw.

"RUN, LORD BLUNDERBUSS!" she replied. "RUN FOR YOUR LIFE!"

"THANK YOU, NANNY!"

The man did just that. He ran away – well, lightly *jogged* away, because he got a stitch.

As for the Abominable Snowman, Nanny felt it best when introducing him to change his name.

"ANIMALS!" she called. "CALM DOWN!"

Because she had saved all their lives, the animals stopped and listened to her.

"Good. Now, there is **no need** to be afraid. Let me introduce you all to our newest friend. This is the Rather **Nice** Snowman!"

"Hello!" chirped the not-at-all frightening monster.

"HELLO!" they all called back.

"GROUP CUDDLE!" said Nanny.

Together, all the animals at **BLUNDERBUSS MANOR** gathered around her for a giant **hug**.

Soon, they turned the old country house into a wildlife park. The star attraction was the Rather Nice Snowman.

As for the Abominable Lord Blunderbuss, he lightly **jogged** all the way back to the **Himalayan mountains.** There the old fool hid in the forest, surviving only on a diet of **lemon-** and **chocolate-flavoured** snow.

"BLEURGH!"

The True Story
of the
LOCH NESS MONSTER

NEARLY A CENTURY AGO, two naughty boys
tumbled out of a cinema. Their eyes blinking in the
daylight, they were in shock and awe. The pair had
watched the greatest film they had ever seen in
their lives.

KING KONG.

It was an epic story about a giant **gorilla** who was stolen from his island home, imprisoned onboard an ocean liner and taken to be put on display in New York City. *KING KONG* ended up escaping and came to a tragic end falling from the Empire State Building.

All this felt like a million miles away from the boys' quiet life on the bonny banks of Loch Ness, one of the largest lochs in Scotland.

Donald and Angus had been friends since before they could remember. Now twelve years old, they spent all day playing together. Angus had a younger sister, Rose, who was only ten. Rose was unable to hear or speak. She was a clever little girl, who loved to devour books about **myths** and **LEGENDS**. Her imagination was so strong that she would write her own stories and illustrate them beautifully.

Ever since they had watched the movie, Angus and Donald's games all involved *KING KONG.* One would pretend to be the giant gorilla scaling the Empire State Building, or, in their case, the ruins of a castle that overlooked the loch. Meanwhile, the other would play at being a pilot in a biplane, delivering the fatal shot that toppled *KING KONG.*

It was the most thrilling game ever.

Sometimes Rose would observe them from a distance and smile at how *silly* the pair looked.

One evening, as they walked home along the edge of the water, Donald looked sad.

"What's the matter?" asked Angus.

Donald was the taller one. Angus was shorter with wonderfully knobbly knees and a fantastic explosion of ginger hair.

"It's silly."

"What's silly?"

"Why can't we live in New York City where they've got monsters as big as skyscrapers?"

This made Angus laugh. "HA! HA! You daft thing!

You do know that **KING KONG** fella isn't real?"

Donald pretended to look shocked. "You're joking!"
Then he couldn't help but smile. "Course I know **KING KONG** isn't real – I am not completely glaikit – but *silly* wouldn't it be marvellous if we had our OWN beastie here in little old Loch Ness?"

"But nothing ever happens here," replied Angus. He picked up a stone and expertly *skimmed* it across the loch.

PING! PING! PING!

They both looked out as the stone bounced and then s a n k with a plop!

The sun was setting. The loch was bathed in a **fiery** glow.

"What would it be?" mused Donald. "Not a giant **gorilla.** They've already done that!"

"Some kind of fish?"

afraid

"Nobody would be feart of a fish."

"Sharks are scary!"

babbling

"Stop blethering! You don't get killer sharks in Loch Ness. No one would believe that!"

There was silence for a moment as both boys thought long and hard.

"I know!" exclaimed Angus. "A dinosaur!"

"A swimming dinosaur!" added Donald.

big

"Like a huge, muckle underwater dinosaur monster!"

"The Loch Ness Monster!" they both cried at once.

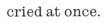

Over the next days and weeks and months, the naughty pair began to hatch a **plan.** If they could make everyone in the world believe that a monster lived in Loch Ness, they would be RICH!

Rose would sometimes tiptoe around the family cottage, and spy on what the boys were doing. However, not being able to hear, it was hard for her to understand what they were up to. But, knowing her brother and his friend, she knew it was mischief.

As it turned out, it was the greatest mischief the world had ever known!

First, Angus and Donald needed to create their own Loch Ness Monster.

Second, they had to fake some photographs of the creature.

Third, they must make sure those photographs were seen in every newspaper in the world.

Fourth, tourists would flock to Loch Ness to try to catch a glimpse of the monster.

Fifth, who would be their tour guides? None other than the two local boys who took the first photograph of the creature!

"That's not all!" said Donald. "Just think of all the tat we could flog!"

"Loch Ness Monster toys!" exclaimed Angus.

"Loch Ness Monster tea towels!"

"Loch Ness Monster tammies!" ← woollen hats

"Loch Ness Monster pencil cases!"

"LOCH NESS MONSTER EVERYTHING!"

So, keeping all this a secret from everyone, including Rose, the two set about putting their *MONSTER PLAN* into action.

In Rose's room, Angus found a big book on dinosaurs. Studying the pages gave Rose *inspiration* for her stories. As she had so many books, she didn't notice it was missing from her shelf at first.

In Angus's bedroom, he and Donald were drawn to the picture of a *plesiosaur.*

"That's what our monster should look like!" exclaimed Donald.

"BINGO!" agreed Angus.

Building a life-sized dinosaur seemed like an impossible task, until the boys realised something. Most of the monster's body would be hidden under the water. They only really needed to build a neck with a head on top, and the arch of its back. These parts they shaped out of wood in Angus's father's workshop and nailed together.

Rose didn't hear the **BANGING** downstairs, or she would have sneaked down to investigate.

With the workshop door locked, Angus and Donald painted the whole thing green.

Finally, they added some eyes and a mouth.

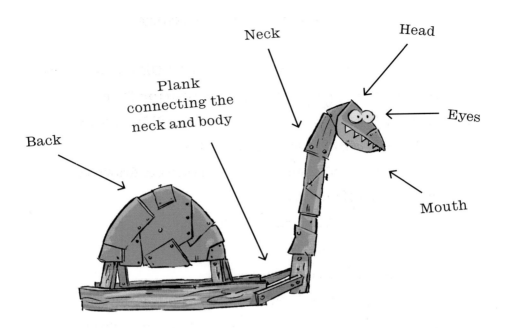

Back

Plank
connecting the
neck and body

Neck

Head

Eyes

Mouth

It was the world's absolute **worst** monster! It wasn't
even real! But the naughty pair thought they could get
away with fooling **everyone!**

One of them would have to swim **underneath** this
contraption, while the other took a photograph. The
water in the loch was *ice-cold* even in the height of
summer, so neither boy wanted to do the swimming part.
However, Angus's father owned a camera, and the boy
insisted only **he** should be allowed to operate it!

So poor Donald had to get into the water at dawn when
no one else was about.

In a loch.

In Scotland.

In winter.

Meanwhile, a smug-looking Angus was standing on the bank of the loch with his father's camera, which he barely knew how to operate.

But he pressed the right button.

CLICK!

They had the shot!

Quickly, they developed the photograph in Angus's father's darkroom. It was grainy and out of focus, but that only added to the mystery. With the print still wet, the pair ran all the way to the offices of the local newspaper.

"HOLD THE FRONT PAGE!" shouted Angus.

It was something he had heard in a movie, and it sounded dramatic.

The wee old lady who ran the *Loch Ness Gazette* woke up from her afternoon snooze.

"What the...?" she spluttered.

"THERE IS A M-M-MONSTER IN THE L-L-LOCH!" shouted Donald, his teeth still chattering from the icy water.

The lady pulled down her spectacles and examined the grainy black-and-white photograph.

"MY GOODNESS ME!" she exclaimed. "We are going to double our readership overnight!"

"How many newspapers do you normally sell?" asked Angus.

"Just the one. To my husband, Jock. But this is big news. I will have to print two!"

The story grew and grew.

First, it was on the front page of the *Loch Ness Gazette*. Then the *Scotsman*. Then the *London Times*. Before long it was on the front page of every newspaper in the world!

After the story broke, everyone around Loch Ness was giddy with excitement. None more so than Rose. Using sign language, she asked her brother, "Please can you show me the monster?"

"No," Angus signed back.

"Why?"

"I just can't. You're only a bairn!" ← child

"But I want to see it. More than anything in the world."

"NO! NOW WHEESHT!"

hush →

Rose was crestfallen. Her own brother was the one who had taken the photograph of the Loch Ness Monster, and yet he wouldn't let her see it with her own eyes.

Only when she was examining the books on her shelf did she realise that the one about dinosaurs was missing. After searching the house, she found it hidden under Angus's bed. Flicking through it, she saw that the *plesiosaur* page was marked with a fold. Rose was heartbroken. Blessed with such a vivid imagination, she wanted to believe in this monster more than anyone.

Was the whole thing a hoax?

However, people in their **thousands** had begun lining the banks of Loch Ness. They had come from all around the world. They jostled with each other for a glimpse of the monster. And, all the time, who was selling them food and drink and souvenirs?

Angus and Donald, of course.

They named the Loch Ness Monster Nessie, and a LEGEND was born.

Over time, many began to doubt the existence of this beast. There were no more sightings. The surface of the loch remained as still as glass. Not even a RIPPLE.

But Angus and Donald didn't care. They had already made a fortune out of the monster tourists.

One night, Rose confronted her brother.

"Did you and Donald make the whole story up?"

"No!" he lied, replying in sign language.

"So there really is a monster?"

"Yes!"

"You saw it with your own eyes?"

"Yes!"

"Promise? You're not havering?" *talking nonsense*

"I promise!"

Rose needed to find out for herself and became the most dedicated monster spotter there was.

As night fell on the loch, the air was colder than snow. All the tourists would troop back to their hotels and guesthouses for the night. Rose always stayed watching and waiting, until she was all but dragged home.

One night, Angus spotted his little sister standing

alone in the cold and felt desperately guilty. If he hadn't lied to her, she would be home in the warm right now.

So, after packing up his suitcase full of Nessie toys, games and novelty underpants, Angus approached his little sister.

freezing cold

"Come on, Rose!" Angus signed. "It's Baltic. We need to go!"

"Tell Mum and Dad I will be home in time for tea!" she signed back.

"But I'm your big brother. I need to look after you."

"I will be fine, Angus. I am old enough to look after myself. Run along and I will be home soon."

Angus felt sick with guilt. But he and Donald had sworn never to tell anyone that the whole thing was a giant hoax.

"Don't be long!" he signed. "You'll catch cold!"

That night there was *magic* in the air. The loch was lit up by the stars.

Despite everything, Rose never stopped believing. And, if you never stop believing, sometimes, just sometimes, your

dreams can come true. ✦ ✦

Because that night a beast rose out of the loch.

It wasn't Angus and Donald's silly wooden model – it was the real-life Loch Ness Monster!

It was far away from a *plesiosaur.*

It was a dragon. A mythical creature.

Beautiful and terrifying in equal measure.

Rose was frozen in fear when she spotted the beast, close to the bank. What's more, it turned its gaze on to her. Rose could feel its breath on her face.

HURR!

The creature inspected Rose with its huge dark eyes. Of course, Rose couldn't scream. Even if she could, no one would hear her. She was all alone.

A smile crossed the monster's face. At first, Rose thought this was a **sinister** smile. One that a crocodile might give before going in for the kill.

But then she saw something in the monster's eyes.

Something warm.

Something gentle.

Something kind.

Something that looked a lot like love.

The monster bowed its head and lowered it, all the way down to her feet. It felt like an **invitation.** Rose stepped on to the monster's head, and then turned round and *slid* down its neck.

WHOOSH!

Her bottom landed on the monster's back.

BOOF!

Rose wrapped her arms round its neck, and in a moment they were off.

SWISH!

The monster took the girl for a tremendous tour of the loch at a splendid speed.

Rose had to hold on tight so she would not fall off.

But she didn't feel frightened.

This was the most **thrilling** moment of her life,